And so here she was. Barely in New York for five seconds and fixed up with a job for just the sort of pinstripe-suited money-man that she had always hated.

The penthouse apartment had its own private lift, and she was discharged into a massive carpeted landing. Disorientated, she wondered whether she was actually *in* the apartment. And, if so, where was the dreaded Matt Strickland?

'Miss Kelly, I take it?'

The sound of his voice shocked her into spinning round, red-faced and feeling as guilty as if he had caught her stealing the family silver.

For a few timeless seconds Tess stared. Every cosy image she had had of Matt Strickland was shattered in an instant. This was six foot two inches of hard-packed alpha male. Suffocatingly masculine.

Cathy Williams is originally from Trinidad, but has lived in England for a number of years. She currently has a house in Warwickshire, which she shares with her husband, Richard, her three daughters, Charlotte, Olivia and Emma, and their pet cat, Salem. She adores writing romantic fiction, and would love one of her girls to become a writer—although at the moment she is happy enough if they do their homework and agree not to bicker with one another!

First published in Great Britain 2011
by Mills & Boon, an imprint of Harlequin (UK) Limited,
Eton House, 18-24 Paradise Road, Richmond, Surrey TW9 1SR

ISBN: 978 0 263 88674 0

Harlequin (UK) policy is to use papers that are natural, renewable and recyclable products and made from wood grown in sustainable forests. The logging and manufacturing process conform to the legal environmental regulations of the country of origin.

Printed and bound in Spain
by Blackprint CPI, Barcelona

HER IMPOSSIBLE BOSS

CHAPTER ONE

WIDE, sensual mouth compressed, Matt stared down at the makeshift CV sitting in front of him. It was difficult to know where to begin. The colourful list of jobs complemented by the even more impressive lack of duration at each one of them told their own story. As did the brief, uninspiring academic profile. In the normal course of events he would have tossed this application into the bin without even bothering to read the sketchy handwritten personal profile at the end. Unfortunately, this was *not* the normal course of events.

He finally looked across his highly polished mahogany desk at the girl perched nervously on the chair facing him.

'Eight jobs.' He pushed himself away from the desk and allowed the lengthening silence to fill in the blanks of what he wanted to say.

Tess Kelly had come to him via a reference from her sister, and, in no position to be choosy, here he now was, interviewing for a nanny for his daughter. From what he could see, not only was Tess Kelly resoundingly lacking in any relevant experience, she was also flighty and academically challenged.

Huge green eyes looked back at him and he followed

her nervous gesture as she chewed her bottom lip. He might have his hands tied, but that didn't mean that he was going to make this process easy for her.

'I know it sounds like a lot…'

'You're twenty-three years old and you've held down eight jobs. I think it's fair to say that it is a lot.'

Tess looked away from the cool dark eyes resting on her. Under his unflinching, assessing gaze, she was finding it impossible to keep still. Why on earth was she here? She had arrived in New York three weeks previously to stay with her sister, with the proviso that she take some time out to consider her options and get her act together. At least those had been the parting words of her parents as they had waved her off at the airport before she'd disappeared across the Atlantic.

'You're twenty-three years old, Tess,' her mother had said firmly, offering her a plate of homemade biscuits to soften the blow, 'and you still don't seem to have any idea what you want to do with your life. Your dad and I would just like to see you settle down. Find something that you enjoy doing—something you might want to stick with for longer than five minutes… Claire knows all the ins and outs of the business world. She'll be able to give you some helpful advice. It would do you good to spend your summer somewhere else…'

No one had mentioned that part of the process would involve getting a job as a nanny. She had never worked with any child in her life before. She couldn't remember having ever expressed the slightest curiosity about working with one. And yet here she was, sitting in front of a man who chilled her to the bone. The very second she had spun round at the sound of his velvety voice, to see him lounging against the doorframe, inspecting her, she had felt a shiver of apprehension skim down her spine. She had prepared herself for someone portly and middle-aged. He was, after all, her sister's boss. He owned the company, he ran it, and according to Claire he took no prisoners. How could he do all that and still be in his early thirties? But he was—and, contrary to all expectations, not only was he young, he also had killer looks. Drop-dead, truly sensational killer looks.

But his emotional detachment was terrifying, and his perfect bone structure proclaimed a face that never cracked a smile. Tess wondered how her sister could work for him without having a nervous breakdown.

'And your academic history… I'm finding it hard to tally your lack of qualifications with your sister's achievements. Claire has a first class degree and is head of my corporate law department. You have…let's count them…six mediocre GCSE grades and a certificate in Foundation Art…'

'Yes, well, I'm not Claire, Mr Strickland.' Two patches of colour appeared on her cheeks. 'Claire and Mary both excelled at school…'

'Mary being…?'

'My other sister. She's a doctor. They were both high-achievers. Not everyone is built along the same lines.' Cheerful by nature, Tess was finding that she *loathed* this man. From his opening words to her— *'You're half an hour late and I don't tolerate lateness.'* —to his sweeping assumption that she was a failure. He hadn't said it in so many words, but it was there, lurking in the cold, disdainful expression behind those bitter chocolate eyes.

'Okay. Let's do away with the formalities and cut to the chase, shall we?' Matt leaned forward and rested his elbows on the desk. 'You're here because I am not in a position of choice. I don't know what, precisely, Claire has told you, but let me clarify. My ex-wife died some months ago and since than I have had full custody of my ten-year-old daughter. In that period she has seen off almost as many nannies as you have seen off jobs. Consequently, the agency I deal with have effectively closed their doors to me. I have three housekeepers, but they are not suitable for the demands of the job. I could look further afield, but frankly this is a three-month posting—and finding a career nanny who is willing to offer herself for such a short period of time will not be easy. Time, Miss Kelly, is of the essence as far as I am concerned. I work huge hours. I have neither the time nor the ability to cover. Your name cropped up. Your sister sings your praises when it comes to your sociability. Ergo, you are here now—despite your glaring shortcomings.'

Not for the first time, Matt considered the train of events that had led to where he was now.

Divorced for eight years, he had been an infrequent spectator to his daughter's life. Catrina, his ex-wife, had removed her to Connecticut a year after their divorce had become final, and had played so many games when it came to making arrangements for him to visit that the years had elapsed without him ever really feeling connected to Samantha. And then, six months ago, Catrina had died in a car accident, and the daughter he had never really known had landed on his doorstep—resentful, grieving, and silently, wilfully hostile.

Nannies, a necessity for him, had come and gone, and he now found himself between a rock and a hard place.

'I'm sorry. I'm *so* sorry. Claire didn't mention details… Your poor, poor daughter…' Tears of sympathy were gathering in the corners of Tess's eyes and she blinked them away. 'I'm not surprised she's finding it difficult to settle down.'

Taken aback by such an emotional response, Matt reached into a drawer in his desk and pulled out a box of tissues, which he handed to her.

'So, whilst you're not my idea of the ideal candidate…' He carried on over the subsiding threat of her tears.

'I guess you're worried because I've had so many jobs over the years…' Tess was prepared to give him the benefit of the doubt. He might be harsh and forbidding, but he was in a difficult position and no doubt justifiably anxious that he take on someone who wouldn't let him down.

'Correct. Samantha would not benefit from someone who decides to stick around for a few days and then walks out because she's bored. Even though there have been a lot of nannies, they have all endeavoured to give it their best shot. Are you capable of that?'

'Yes. Yes, I am.' She looked at him. Despite the unforgiving nature of his expression, a little voice whispered, he really was very good-looking—beautiful, almost. Suddenly hot and bothered, she looked away, twisting the tissue between her fingers.

'Convince me.'

'I beg your pardon?'

'I may not be in a position to pick and choose, Miss

Kelly, but I would still like you to persuade me that I am not about to make a mistake with you. Your sister may well sing your praises, and I trust Claire, but…' He shrugged and relaxed back. 'Persuade me…'

'I wouldn't leave anyone in the lurch. I really wouldn't, Mr Strickland.' She leaned forward, her face flushed and sincere. 'I know you think that I'm probably not very good at sticking to anything. Well, actually,' she confessed, 'my family would all probably agree with you. But I've actually been indispensable in many of my past jobs. I've never let anyone *down*—not really. No, not at all, come to think of it. Even when I quit the receptionist's job at Barney and Son, Gillian was there to take over. To be honest, I think they were all a little relieved when I decided to leave. I was forever transferring people to the wrong department…'

'Let's try and stick to the theme.'

'Yes. Well, what I'm trying to say is that you can trust me with your daughter. I won't let you down.'

'Even though you have no experience in the field and might get bored with the company of a ten-year-old child?'

'I don't think kids are boring! Do you?'

Matt flushed darkly. *Was* he bored in Samantha's company? He had precious little experience in that area to provide a qualified answer. His relationship with his daughter was fraught at best. They conversed intermittently, and across a seemingly unbreachable chasm. She was sulky and uncommunicative, and he knew that he was not a feelings person.

Matt dismissed that brief moment of intense introspection.

'So how would you plan on looking after her?' He pushed the conversation forward and focused on her.

She had a fascinatingly transparent face. Right now, giving his question some thought, she was lost in a slight frown, her lips parted, her apple-green eyes distant. Tess Kelly wasn't the sort of woman he had been expecting. Claire was tall, brisk, efficient, and permanently attired in a suit. The girl sitting opposite him was a living, breathing testimony to the power of misconception. She looked as though she had never been anywhere near a suit and her hair…

No fashionably tailored bob, but really, *really* long. Several times he had been tempted to angle himself so that he could see just how long for himself.

'Well…I guess there are the usual sights. Museums, art galleries. And then there's the cinema, the zoo… I love Central Park. We could go there. I'm sure she'll be missing the familiarity of her home and all her friends, so I'll make sure to keep her busy and occupied.'

'And then there's the matter of schoolwork.'

Tess blinked and looked at him in confusion. 'What schoolwork?' she asked, perplexed. 'It's the holidays.'

'Samantha's education was severely disrupted because of Catrina's death, as you can imagine. More so when she came to New York. There seemed little point in registering her for a school here, which she wouldn't be attending on a permanent basis, and the tutors I employed for her came and went as regularly as the nannies. Consequently there are gaps in her learning which will have to be addressed before she sits exams at the beginning of September for her new school.'

'Okaayyy...and where do I fit in?'

Tess continued to look at him blankly and he clicked his tongue with impatience. '*You're* going to have to take charge there.'

'Me?' Tess squeaked in consternation. '*I* can't become a tutor! You've seen my application form! You've *made fun* of my lack of qualifications!'

The thought of trying to teach anything to someone else horrified her. She wasn't academic. She became nervous just thinking about textbooks. The youngest of three girls, she had grown up in the shadow of her clever sisters, and from an early age had dealt with the problem by simply opting out. No one could accuse her of being thick if she simply refused to compete, could they? And she had known that there was no way that she could ever have competed with either Claire or Mary. How on earth could he expect her to suddenly become a *tutor*?

'I'm sorry to have wasted your time, Mr Strickland,' she said, standing up abruptly. 'If teaching is part of the job, then I'm going to have to turn down the position. I...I can't. Claire and Mary are the brainy ones. I'm not. I've never been to university. I never even wanted to go. I did a foundation course in Art when I was sixteen, and that's the extent of my qualifications. You need someone else.'

Matt looked at her narrowly and allowed her to ramble on. Then, very calmly, he told her to sit.

'I'm getting the picture about your academic qualifications or lack of them. You hated school.'

'I didn't *hate* school.' Having not wanted the job to start with, Tess now realised that she did. His daughter's plight had touched her. The thought of her being so young, and dependent on a father who was obviously a workaholic, tugged at her heartstrings. For the first time she really wanted to get involved. 'I'm just no good when it comes to textbooks.'

'I have no time for people who wave a white flag and concede defeat before they've even given something a fair chance,' Matt said bracingly. 'I'm not asking you to teach to degree level. I'm asking you to tutor Samantha in some of the basics—maths, english, sciences. If you want to persuade me that you're interested in taking on this job, then you're going about it the wrong way.'

'I'm just being honest! If…if you don't want to employ any more tutors for your daughter, then why don't *you* help her with her schoolwork?' She faltered. 'You run a business, so you must be qualified…or maybe you don't need maths and English in what you do…? Some children don't cope well with home-tutoring. Perhaps your daughter is one of those…'

'Samantha could cope very well with home-tutoring,' Matt said shortly, 'if she was prepared to put effort into it. But she's not. She might benefit more from teaching in a less structured manner. And, no, there is no way that I can help out. I barely have time to sleep. I leave this apartment at seven-thirty in the morning, which is an hour later than I used to before Samantha arrived, and I try and make it back by eight in the evening when I'm not away. Which is a push at the best of times.'

Tess was distracted sufficiently from her own agonising to shoot him a look of frank horror. 'You work from seven-thirty in the morning to eight at night? Every day?'

'I cut myself some slack on the weekends.' Matt shrugged. He could think of no one who would find anything out of the ordinary about those working hours. The high-fliers in his company—and there were a lot of them—routinely had punishing schedules and thought nothing of it. They were paid fabulous sums of money and quid pro quo, after all.

'What does that mean?'

'Where are you going with this?' Matt asked irritably. 'You're straying from the topic.'

'I'm sorry,' Tess breathed. 'I just feel so sorry for you.'

'Come again?' Matt could hardly credit what he was hearing. If they haven't been discussing something so important, he would have laughed. Never, but *never*, had anyone *felt sorry* for him. Quite the opposite. Being born into a legacy of wealth, power and influence had opened a thousand doors. Without siblings, the task of taking hold of the family fortunes had fallen onto his shoulders, and not only had he looked after the billions but he had gone several steps further and dramatically increased their worth. He had diversified and invested in areas his father would never have dreamed of, and in so doing had attained a position of impenetrable power. He was virtually untouchable. The economic and financial crises that had seen off so many of his rivals had skirted harmlessly around him. It was a situation he had engineered, and one he enjoyed.

'I can't think of anything more horrible than being slave to a job, but you're right. I'm getting off the subject.

I was just wondering why you didn't cover the school-work with Samantha yourself if you think that the home-tutoring doesn't work, but I can see that you don't have the time.'

Was it his imagination or was there a hint of gentle criticism there?

'Good. I'm glad we agree.'

'Would you mind me asking you something?' Tess ventured, clearing her throat. When he tilted his head to one side she said, tentatively, 'When do you have time for your daughter, if you work such long hours?'

Matt stared at her in disbelief. The directness of the question put him soundly on the back foot—as did the fact that he was seldom in a position of having to field direct questions of a personal nature. Women just *didn't* go there. But she was waiting for an answer.

'I fail to see what this has to do with the job,' he said stiffly.

'Oh, but it has lots to do with the job! I mean, I'm sure you have special times set aside, and I would want to know that so that I didn't intrude. I just don't see where those special times would fit in if you're working from seven-thirty to eight every day, and only taking a bit of time off over the weekends.'

'I don't have a structure for the time I spend with Samantha.' His voice was cold and uninviting. 'We very often go to The Hamptons so that she can see her grand-parents on the weekend.'

'That's lovely.' Tess was unconvinced.

'And now that we've covered that, let's move on to your hours.' He tapped his pen absently on the desk, beating a staccato rhythm that made her feel as though she was being cross-examined rather than interviewed. 'I'll expect you to be here every morning no later than seven-thirty.'

'Seven-thirty?'

'Does that pose a problem?'

Torn between truth and tact, Tess remained silent until he prompted, with raised eyebrows, 'I'm taking that as a *no.* It's a requirement of the job. I could occasionally request one of my housekeepers to cover for you in an emergency, but I would hope that the occasion doesn't arise.'

Tess had always been punctual at all her jobs—the very many she had had over the years—but it had to be said that none of them had required her to wake up at the crack of dawn. She wasn't an early-morning person. Somehow she knew that was a concept he would never be able to understand. She wondered whether he ever slept.

'Do all your employees work long hours?' she asked faintly, and for some reason Matt had the strongest inclination to burst out laughing. Her appalled look said it all.

'They don't get paid the earth to clock-watch,' he said seriously. 'Are you telling me that you've never worked overtime in your life before?'

'I've never had to,' Tess told him earnestly. 'But then again, I've never been paid the earth for anything I've done. Not that I mind. I've never been that interested in money.'

Matt was intrigued, against his will. Was this woman from the same planet as he was? He should stick to the programme, but he found himself strangely willing to digress.

'Really?' he said with scepticism. 'In that case, I applaud you. You're one of a kind.'

Tess wondered whether he was being sarcastic, but then, looking around her at the luxurious surroundings of his penthouse, where the old sat comfortably with the new and every hanging on the walls and rug strewn on the floor screamed wealth, she realised that he would be genuinely mystified at her indifference to money.

It had very quickly struck her, the second she had walked through the front door of his apartment, that Matt Strickland was a man who moved in circles so far removed from her own that they barely occupied the same stratosphere. The people he mixed with would share the same exalted lifestyle, and it was a lifestyle that could not be achieved without an unswerving dedication to the art of making money.

But Tess had been telling the absolute truth when she had told him that money didn't interest her. If it had, she might have been a little more driven when it came to a career.

Nor did she have a great deal of respect for someone who put money at the top of their list. Someone, in short, like Matt Strickland. Even though she could appreciate that he was clever and ambitious, there was a hard, cutting edge to him that left her cold.

She sneaked a quick look at that striking face, and her heart beat a little faster and a little harder in her chest.

'You're not saying anything. I take it that you disapprove of all of this?' He gestured sweepingly with one hand. This was a woman, he realised, whose silences were as revealing as the things she said. It was a refreshing trait.

'It's all very comfortable.' Tess tiptoed around telling him the absolute truth—which was that expensive furnishings and investment paintings all came at a price.

'But…?'

'I prefer small and cosy,' she admitted. 'My parents' house is small and cosy. Obviously, not *that* small. There were five of us growing up. But I think that their entire house would fit into just a bit of this apartment.'

'You still live at home with them?' His sharp ears had picked up on the intonation in her voice and his curiosity was instantly roused. What was a twenty-three-year-old woman still doing living at home? And, he noted distractedly, a strikingly pretty twenty-three-year-old girl? Huge green eyes dominated a heart-shaped face that even in moments of thought carried an air of animation. Her long hair was the colour of caramel, and…

His eyes drifted lazily downwards to the full breasts pushing lushly against a small cropped vest, the silver of flat stomach just visible between the vest and the faded jeans that moulded slim legs.

Annoyed at being distracted, Matt stood up and began to prowl through his office. Originally a library, it was still dominated by the hand-made wooden bookcase that stretched along the entire length of the back wall. A rich Oriental rug, handed down through the generations, covered most of the wooden floor. The only modern introductions were the paintings on the walls and, of course, the high-tech paraphernalia essential to his work.

'I...at the moment I do,' Tess mumbled, with sudden awkward embarrassment.

'And you've *never* lived on your own?'

The incredulity in his voice made her spin round to glare at him defensively. She decided that he really was truly hateful. Hateful and judgemental.

'There was never a need for me to live on my own!' she said in a high pitched voice. 'I didn't go to university, and there was no point looking for somewhere to rent when it was just as convenient for me to carry on living at home.' As if it were spelt out in bold neon lettering, she was appalled to hear with her own ears just how hopeless that made her sound. Twenty-three and still living with Mum and Dad. Angry tears threatened to push their way to the surface and she blinked rapidly, forcing them back.

'Remarkable.'

'Most of my friends still live at home. It's not that remarkable.'

'And you never felt the need to spread your wings and do something different? Or did you give up and wave the white flag before you could get around to challenging yourself?'

Tess was shocked at the strength of her reaction. She had never shown any inclination towards violence before, but she could easily have leapt out of her chair and thrown something at him. Instead, she subsided into angry silence. Her entire nervous system picked up pace as he circled her and then leant down, arms on either side of her chair, effectively caging her in.

'I don't see what my home life has to do with this

job,' she breathed jerkily, looking anywhere but at the brown muscular forearms on either side of her.

'I'm trying to get a measure of you as a person. You're going to be responsible for the welfare of my daughter. You come with no references from a professional agency. I need to find out that you're not going to prove a liability. Shall I tell you what I've concluded so far?'

Tess wondered whether she had a choice. Had her tongue been able to unglue itself from the roof of her mouth, she might have summoned up the courage to say something along those lines, but sarcastic rejoinders weren't her forte and his proximity was wreaking havoc with her composure. Her skin was tingling, and she felt as though she was having to drag the oxygen into her lungs in order to breathe.

It was a relief when he pushed himself away from her chair and resumed his place behind the desk.

'You're lazy. You're unfocused. You're lacking in self-confidence and you've been perfectly happy to carry on being that way.' He enunciated each derogatory bullet point with the cold precision of a judge passing sentence on a criminal. 'You still live at home and it doesn't seem to have occurred to you somewhere along the way that your parents might not be as happy with that situation as you are. You pick jobs up and you put them down again because you don't want to be stretched. I'm no psychologist, but I'm guessing that it's because you think you can't fail at anything if you never bother to give your all to it.'

'That's horrible.' Unfortunately there were elements of truth in some of what he had said, and for that she hated him. 'Why are you interviewing me for this job if you have such a low opinion of me?' she asked on a whisper. 'Or has the interview ended? Is this your way of telling me that I haven't got the job? Yes, it is. And, that being the case—' Tess inhaled one deep breath that steadied her fraying nerves '—then I can tell you what I think of you too!' She looked at him with stormy green eyes and drew herself upright in her chair. 'I think that you're arrogant and rude. You think that just because you…you make a lot of money and grew up with a lot of money you can treat people any way you want to and be as offensive as you want to be. I think that it's awful that you obviously work so hard that you have no time left over to give your daughter—who *needs* you! Or maybe you just don't know *how* to give yourself to anyone else!'

Her breathing was jerky from the effort of pouring emotions she'd never known she possessed into what was, for her, an all-out shouting match. The worst of it was that she didn't feel good about herself—even though she had spoken her mind, and even though speaking her mind should have achieved some sort of healthy cleansing.

'And I'm *not* lazy,' she concluded, deflating like a balloon with its air suddenly released. 'If that's all.' She stood up and tried to gather some shreds of dignity. 'I'll be on my way.'

Matt smiled, and Tess was so flustered by that smile that she remained rooted to the spot, dithering as though her legs had forgotten how to work.

'You have fire. I like that. You're going to need some of it when it comes to handling my daughter.'

'Wha—at?'

He waved her down into the chair and leaned back. 'It's healthy to hear a little criticism now and again. I can't remember the last time anyone raised their voice in my presence.' Particularly, he could have added, when it came to women. As if a switch had been turned on in his head, he suddenly keenly noted the fading pinkness in her cheeks. Her hair had fallen forward and was now spread over her shoulders, falling like spun silk over her breasts, almost down to her waist. She was regaining some of her lost composure but her breasts were still heaving.

He was shocked by the sudden responsive stirring in his loins. God, he had a girlfriend! An extremely clever, very high-powered girlfriend. One who understood completely the constraints of his job because they mirrored her own! They were on the same wavelength. She was diametrically, radically and dramatically the opposite to the elfin creature with the big green eyes sitting opposite him. Vicky Burns was focused, driven, and university-educated to the highest possible level.

So why the hell was he wondering what Tess Kelly looked like with her clothes off and only her long, long hair to cover her modesty?

He wrote a figure on a piece of paper and slid it across the desk to her.

Tess leant forward, and of their own accord his eyes strayed to the cleavage she revealed as she reached for the paper.

With a sigh of pure frustration Matt rubbed his eyes and half swivelled his chair, so that he was facing the vast windows of the library, framed with their heavy velvet curtains. It was a safer sight than the one his rebellious eyes had been absorbing.

'This is too much, Mr Strickland. I couldn't possibly accept.'

'Don't be ridiculous!' Annoyed with himself for his uncustomary lapse of self-control, Matt made his voice sharper than intended. He reluctantly turned to look at her. 'It's perfectly reasonable. You're being asked to do a hugely important job, and for that money…well, consider yourself on a learning curve as far as overtime goes. There's just one more thing. You'll have to dress the part.' He flushed darkly at the confusion on her face. 'Looser clothing. It's more practical in this heat. Particularly if you intend on doing…er…outdoor activities…'

'But I don't have any loose clothing.'

'Then you'll have to buy some. It's not an insurmountable problem, Tess. You will have access to an account for all expenses to do with the job. Make use of it.' He stood up, back in control of his wayward body, and waited as she scrambled to her feet, gathering her satchel which she slung over her shoulder.

'Now it's time for you to meet my daughter. She's upstairs in her bedroom. I'll show you to the kitchen. You can familiarise yourself with it. Make yourself a cup of coffee. I'll bring her down.'

Tess nodded. After her gruelling interview, from which she was still reeling, the prospect of meeting Samantha wasn't as daunting as she would have expected. What could be more full-on than her father had been?

The apartment, sprawling in all directions, occupied

the entire top two floors of the building. Matt showed her into a kitchen which was as stunningly modern as the rest of the apartment was shamelessly and opulently old. Granite surfaces positively gleamed, and were completely bare of any of the normal clutter associated with day-to-day life. Tess foresaw problems should she attempt to do any cooking with her charge. She would be terrified of ruining the show home look.

'Make yourself at home,' he insisted, while she continued to look around her with the lost expression of someone suddenly transported to foreign territory.

For a few seconds Matt watched her with rare amusement. 'It doesn't bite,' he said, and Tess flushed. 'There's tea and coffee in one of the cupboards, and in the fridge…' he indicated something sleek that was camouflaged to look like the rest of the kitchen '…there should be milk. My housekeepers make sure that the kitchen is stocked, especially now that Samantha's around. If you're lucky, you might even locate some biscuits somewhere.'

'You mean you don't *know* where things are in your own kitchen?'

Matt grinned, and Tess had a disconcerting window into what this man would look like shorn of his arrogance. Not just beautiful, but dangerously, horribly sexy.

She lowered her eyes as a new, prickly feeling undermined her still shaky composure.

'Terrible, isn't it?' He was still grinning and moving towards the door. He raised his eyebrows. 'Maybe you could work that one into the next speech you give me about my shortcomings.'

Tess smiled weakly back, but somewhere in a part of her she hardly recognised warning bells were beginning to ring—although what that meant she had no idea.

CHAPTER TWO

'WELL? *Well?* What did you think? Have you got the job?'

Claire was waiting for her. Tess had barely had time to insert her key into the front door and there she was, pulling open the door, her face alight with curiosity.

What did she think of Matt Strickland? Tess tried her best to sum up a guy who represented everything she so studiously avoided. Too rich, too arrogant, too stuffy. When her mind strayed to the peculiar way he had made her feel, she reined it back in.

'Can you believe he didn't want me showing up in tight clothing?'

'He's your boss. He can dictate your wardrobe. Do you think *we're* allowed to show up to work in ripped jeans?' Claire pointed out reasonably. 'Move on. Impressions of the apartment?'

'Barely had time to notice.' Tess sighed. 'I've never had such a long interview. I could tell you all about his office, but that's about it. Oh—and the kitchen. I *did* notice that his apartment is the size of a ship, though, and I'm not sure about his taste in art. There were lots of paintings of landscapes and random strangers.'

'That would be his family,' Claire surmised thoughtfully. 'Classy.'

'Really? You think?'

'And finally impressions of the daughter?'

No one had known that he even *had* a daughter, so private was Matt Strickland, and so far he hadn't brought her into the office once!

Tess wondered what there was to tell—considering she hadn't actually met the child. She had waited in the kitchen for what had seemed an unreasonable length of time, and Matt had finally returned in a foul temper and informed her that Samantha had locked herself in her bedroom and was refusing to leave it.

Tess had sipped her tea, distractedly helped herself to her fifth biscuit, absentmindedly gazed at her feet, which had been propped up on a kitchen chair in front of her and pondered the fact that, however powerful, self-assured and downright arrogant Matt Strickland was, there was still at least one person on the face of the earth who was willing to ignore him completely.

'You shouldn't have locks on the doors,' she had informed him thoughtfully. 'We were never allowed to when we were growing up. Mum was always petrified that there would be a fire and she would have no way of getting in.'

He had looked at her as though she had been speaking another language, and only later had she realised that he would have had no real experience of all the small details involved in raising a child.

'So, Monday looks as though it's going to be fun,' she finally concluded now. 'Samantha doesn't want to know, plus I have to be there by seven-thirty. You know how hopeless I am at waking up early…'

Which earned her a look of such filthy warning from Claire that she decided to back off from further complaints on the subject. Of course she would do her very best to wake at the crack of dawn. She would set her alarm, and she would set her phone—but she knew that she might easily sleep through both. What if she did?

She still remembered all the choice words he had used to describe her, and her fact was still worrying at the problem when, the following evening, she answered the landline to hear Matt's dark, smooth voice at the other end of the phone.

Immediately Tess was hurled back to his apartment and that first sight of him, lounging against the doorframe, looking at her.

'You've probably got the wrong sister,' Tess said as soon as he had identified himself—as though there had been *any* chance of her not recognising that voice of his. 'Claire's having a bath, but I'll tell her you called.'

'I called to speak to you,' Matt informed her smoothly. 'Just to remind you that I'll be expecting you at seven-thirty sharp tomorrow morning.'

'Of course I'm going to be there! You can count on me. I'm going to be setting a number of gadgets to make sure I don't oversleep.'

At the other end of the line Matt felt his lips twitch, but he wasn't about to humour her. He got the distinct impression that most people humoured Tess Kelly. There was something infectious about her warmth. However, when it came to his daughter, a stern angle was essential.

'Hello? Are you still there?'

'I am, and to help ease you into punctuality I'll be sending a car for you. It'll be there at seven. You forgot to leave me your mobile number.'

'My mobile number?'

'I need to be able to contact you at all times. Remember, you'll be in charge of my daughter.'

Unaccustomed to being reined in, Tess immediately softened. Of *course* he would want to have her mobile number! He might not be demonstrative when it came to his daughter—not in the way that her parents had always been demonstrative with *her*—but keeping tabs on the nanny showed just how important it was for him to know the whereabouts of Samantha at all times.

She rattled it off, and turned to find Claire looking at her with a grin.

'Step one in being a responsible adult! Be prepared to be answerable to someone else! Matt's a fair guy. He expects a lot from the people who work for him, but he gives a lot back in return.'

'I don't like bossy people,' Tess objected automatically.

'You mean you like people who don't lay down any rules to speak of and just allow you to do whatever you want. The joys of being the baby of the family!'

Tess had always been perfectly happy with that description in the past. Now she frowned. Wasn't the unspoken rider to that description *irresponsible*? Her parents had shipped her out to New York so that she could learn some lessons about growing up from her sister. Was it their way of easing her out of the family nest? Had Matt been unknowingly right with his observations? Taking on the job of looking after someone else's child—a child who had already been through a lot and clearly had issues with her father—was not the job for someone who refused to be responsible. Matt Strickland was prepared to give her a chance in the face of some pretty strong evidence that she wasn't up to the task. Being labelled *the baby of the family* no longer seemed to sit quite right.

She had half expected to arrive the following morning and find herself taking orders from one of those mysterious people he had mentioned who would be there to pick up the slack, but in fact, after her luxurious chauffeured drive, during which she'd taken the opportunity to play tourist and really look at some of the sights from air-conditioned comfort, she found herself being greeted by Matt himself.

The weekend had done nothing to diminish his impact. This time he was dressed for work. A dark suit, white shirt and some hand-tailored shoes—a combination that should have been a complete turn off, but which instead just seemed to elevate his sexiness to ridiculous levels.

'I wasn't expecting you to be here,' Tess said, immediately taken aback.

'I live here—or had you forgotten?' He stood aside and she scuttled past him, weirdly conscious of her body in a way that was alien to her.

Under slightly less pressure now, she had her first opportunity to really appreciate her surroundings. It was much more impressive than she could ever have dreamt. Yes, the place was vast, and, yes, the paintings were uniformly drab—even if the portraits *were* of his family members—but the décor was exquisite. Where she might have expected him to err in favour of minimalism, with maybe just the odd leather sofa here and there and lots of chrome, his apartment was opulent. The patina of the wooden floor was rich and deep, and the rugs were old and elaborate. A galleried landing looked down on the immense space below, and stretching the full height of the walls were two windows which, she could now see, offered a tantalising view of Manhattan. The sort of view to which most normal mortals could only aspire via the tourist route.

'Wow! I didn't really take much notice of your apartment the last time I was here. Well, office and kitchen aside.' She stood in one spot, circling slowly. 'Sorry,' she offered to no one in particular, 'I know it's rude to stare, but I can't help myself.' Her eyes were round like saucers, and for the first time in a long time he fully appreciated the privileges to which he had been born.

'Most of the things in here have been handed down to me,' he said, when she had eventually completed her visual tour and was looking at him. 'In fact, I could trace the provenance of nearly everything here. How was the drive over?'

'Brilliant. Thank you.'

'And you're ready to meet Samantha?'

'I'm sorry I didn't get to meet her last time,' Tess said with a rush of sympathy.

Matt, eager to get the day under way, because he had back-to-back meetings, paused. 'Like I said, she's been through a very rough time. It can be difficult to get through to her sometimes.'

'How awful for you. I would have thought that she would have clung to you after her mother's death.'

'Some situations are not always straightforward,' Matt informed her stiffly. 'I don't see you with any books.'

'Books?' Tess was still trying to figure out what *'not always straightforward'* might mean.

'Schoolbooks,' he said patiently. 'I hope you haven't forgotten that teaching is going to be part of your duties with Samantha?'

'Not on day one, surely?'

'I'm not a believer in putting off for tomorrow what can be done today.'

'Yes, well… I thought that I would get to know her first, before I start trying to teach her the importance of fractions and decimals…'

'Ah. I'm glad to see that you've dropped your defeatist approach and got with the programme!'

'I don't have a defeatist approach! Really I don't.' She had thought a lot about what he had said to her, about her waving a white flag, and decided that he had been way off target. She had always firmly believed herself capable of doing anything. Why else would she have attempted so many varied jobs in the past?

Matt held up his hand to silence her. 'No matter. Samantha's collection of tutors have left a number of books over the course of the past few months. You'll find them in the study. Most are untouched,' he added, his mouth tightening. 'I'm hoping that you prove the exception to the rule.'

'I *did* warn you that I'm not academic…'

'I've tried the academics,' Matt pointed out. 'None

of them worked out. Why do you keep running yourself down?'

'I don't.'

'If you insist on labelling yourself as stupid then don't be surprised when the world decides to agree with you.'

'Wait just a minute!'

He had spun around to lead the way, but now he turned slowly on his heels and looked at her with mild curiosity.

'I'm not *stupid*.' Tess had had time to realise that she couldn't cave in to his much stronger, more dominant personality. It wasn't in her nature to make a fuss, but she would have to stand firm on what she believed or let him ride roughshod over her. 'I could have got very good grades, as it happens.'

'Then why didn't you? Was it easier to fail for lack of trying rather than risk trying to compete with your brilliant sisters and not do quite as well? Okay, I withdraw my remark about your being lazy, but if you want to prove your abilities to me then you've got to step up to the plate. Stop apologising for your lack of academic success and start realising the only thing I care about is that you drop the assumption that you can't teach my daughter. She's in the kitchen, by the way.'

Behind him, Tess quietly bristled. While he explained the working hours of his various housekeepers, who took it in turns to come in during the week to ensure that his apartment was never allowed to accumulate a speck of dust, Tess mulled over what he had said like a dog with a bone. She had blithely gone through life doing as she liked, only half listening to her parents' urgings that she settle down and focus. Claire and Mary were focused. In her own good-natured way she had stubbornly refused to be pushed into a way of life which she thought she couldn't handle. No one had ever bluntly said the things that Matt had said to her, or implied that she was a coward, scared of looking like a failure next to her sisters. She told herself that he knew nothing about her—but his words reverberated in her head like a nest of angry wasps.

She nearly bumped into him when he stopped at the kitchen door. She stepped past him to see her charge sitting at the kitchen table, hunched over a bowl of cereal which she was playing with—filling the spoon with milk, raising it high above the bowl and then slowly tilting the milk back in, unconcerned that half of it was splashing onto the fine grainy wood of the table.

Tess didn't know what she had expected. One thing she really *hadn't* expected was, glancing sideways, to see the shuttered look of pained confusion on Matt's face, and for a few powerful seconds she was taken aback by the burst of sympathy she felt for him.

He was tough and uncompromising and, yes, judgemental of her in a way that left her trembling with anger—yet in the face of his daughter he literally didn't know what to do.

Frankly, nor did she. Stubborn, sulky ten year olds had never featured even on her horizon.

'Samantha. Look at me!' He shoved his hands in his pockets and frowned. 'This is Tess. I told you about her. She's going to be your new nanny.'

Samantha greeted this by propping her chin in her hands and yawning widely. She was probably wearing the most expensive clothes money could buy, but Tess had never seen a child dressed with such old-fashioned lack of taste. Clumpy brown sandals and a flowered sleeveless frock. Silk, from the look of it. What ten-year-old ever wore silk? Her long hair was braided into two plaits with, of all things, ribbons neatly tied into bows at the ends. She was dark-haired, like her father, with the same stubborn, aristocratic set to her features. She would doubtless be a beauty in time, but just at the moment her face was sullen and set.

Tess cleared her throat and took a couple of steps forward. 'Samantha! Hi! Okay, you really don't have to look at me if you don't want to…' She giggled nervously, which earned her a sneaky glance, although the spoon and milk routine was still in full force. 'But I'm new to this place so…' She frantically thought of the one thing she and a ten-year-old girl might have in common. 'Do you fancy exploring the shops with me? My sister doesn't wear the same stuff that I do, and I'm far too scared to venture into some of those department stores without someone to hold my hand…'

'Well, it went okay.'

This was the debriefing. When Matt had called her on her mobile, to tell her that he would expect daily reports of progress, she had been at a loss for words. But expect it he did. In his office. Six sharp, after she had handed over her charge to Betsy, the girl who came in to prepare the evening meal.

The very same car that had collected her in the morning had duly collected her from his apartment and delivered her, like a parcel, to his offices, which occupied some prime real estate in downtown Manhattan.

Having seen where he lived, Tess had been more blasé about where he worked. She'd been swept up twenty-eight storeys and hadn't been surprised to find that his office occupied half of the entire floor, with its own sitting room, meeting room, and a massive outer office with chairs and plants, where a middle-aged woman had been busy packing up to go home.

'Define *okay*.' He leaned back into his leather chair and folded his hands behind his head. 'Take a seat.'

He could hardly believe how easily and effortlessly she had managed to break the ice with Samantha. Compared to the other nannies he had hired, who had smiled stiffly and tried to shake hands and had thereby seemed to seal their fate.

Tess shrugged. 'We're still a long way from being pals, but at least she didn't give me my marching orders.'

'She spoke to you?'

'I asked her questions. She answered some of them.' His low opinion of her still rankled, but she would rise above that if only to prove to herself that she could. 'She hates her wardrobe. I think we bonded there. I'm sorry but I'm going to have to turn down your request to purchase "loose" clothing. I can't take your daughter shopping for young, trendy stuff and then buy drab, tired stuff for myself…'

'Young, trendy stuff?'

'Do you know that she's never owned a pair of ripped jeans?'

'Ripped jeans?'

'Or trainers. I mean proper trainers—not the sort you get for school sports.'

'What *are* proper trainers?'

Matt looked at her. She was flushed, her skin rosy and dewy from walking in the heat, and her hair was up in a high ponytail with long caramel strands escaping around her face. In every conceivable way she was the complete antithesis of any woman he had ever gone out with—including his ex-wife. Vicky, his girlfriend, was striking, but in a controlled, intelligent, vaguely *handsome* way, with short brown hair and high cheekbones, and a dress code that consisted almost entirely of smart suits and high heels. And Catrina, while not a career woman, had descended from old money and had always dressed with subtle, refined, understated glamour. Cashmere and pearls, and elegant knee-length skirts.

He could easily believe that Samantha had never owned a pair of ripped jeans, or faded jeans, or possibly even *any* jeans. As far as he could remember neither had his ex-wife.

He felt his imagination do the unthinkable and begin to break its leash once more, throwing up all sorts of crazy images of the fresh faced girl in front of him.

She was telling him about *'proper trainers'* and he was appalled to discover that he was barely taking in a word she was saying. Instead, he was fighting to dismiss thoughts of what she looked like out of those tight jeans and that small green vest with its indistinct logo of a rock band. It was a primitive urge that had no place in his rigidly controlled world.

'Anyway, I hope you don't mind, but I bought her

one or two things. Trainers, jeans, a few tops from the market…'

'You bought her stuff *from a market*?'

'A lot trendier. Oh, gosh, I can tell from your expression that you don't approve. Don't you ever go to a market to shop?' It was an innocuous question, but for some reason it shifted the atmosphere between them. Just a small, barely noticeable shift, but she was suddenly and uncomfortably aware of his almost black eyes resting on her, and the way her body was responding to his stare.

'I've never been to a market in my life.'

'Well, you don't know what you're missing. One of my friends used to work at a market on the weekends, before she went to college to do a course in jewellery-making. I know a lot about them. Quite a bit of what gets sold is imported rubbish, but some of it's really, really good. Handmade. In fact, I thought at one point that *I* could go into that line of business…' Her cheeks were bright with enthusiasm.

'Never mind. You're here now,' Matt said briskly. 'Tell me what your plans are for the rest of the week. Have you had a chance to discuss the business of schoolwork with her?'

'Not yet…it's only been one day! I *did* glance at those books you mentioned, though…when we got back to the apartment and Samantha was having a bath…'

'And?'

Tess opened her mouth to let him know in advance that she had never been that good at the sciences, and then thought better of it. 'And I suppose I can handle some of it.'

'That's the spirit! Now all we have to do is devise a curriculum…'

'She's nervous about going to school here,' Tess blurted out. 'Has she told you that?'

Matt shifted uncomfortably in his chair. 'I hope you reassured her that there is nothing to worry about.' He papered over the fact that he and Samantha had barely had *any* meaningful conversations since she had arrived in Manhattan.

'It's *your* job to reassure her of that.' Tess looked at him squarely in the eyes. Confrontation had always been something she had studiously avoided. She could remember many an argument between her sisters, both intent on emerging the winner, and had long ago reached the conclusion that nothing was worth the raised voices and the heated exchanges—except she wasn't going to duck under the radar now and assume responsibility for something she knew wasn't hers.

'I've been thinking…' she ventured tentatively.

'Should I be alarmed?'

'You have all these rules that I'm supposed to follow…'

Matt threw back his head and laughed, and then, when he had sobered up, directed a grim look at her. 'That's what normally happens when you do a job for someone else. I've taken a big risk on you, and you're being richly rewarded, so don't imagine for a second that you can start trying to negotiate on some of the things you're supposed to do.'

'I'm not trying to negotiate anything!' Tess said heatedly. 'I just think that if there are all these rules for me, then there should be some rules for you.'

Matt looked at her incredulously, and then he burst out laughing again.

'What's so funny?'

'What *you* seem to consider rules most people would consider their job description. Is that how you approached all those jobs you had? With the attitude that you weren't prepared to work for anyone unless they were prepared to bend their rules to accommodate *you*?'

'Of course not.' When things had become too tedious she had simply given up, she thought uncomfortably. 'And I'm not trying to bend any rules.' What *was* it about this man that fired her up and made her argumentative?

'Okay. Spit it out, then.'

'I made a little list.' She had scribbled it in the car on the way over. Several times she had ever asked Stanton, the driver, what he remembered about his childhood—what stood out in his head about the things he had done with his parents that he had really enjoyed.

Matt took the list and read it through. Then he read it again, his expression of disbelief growing by the minute.

'"Monday night,"' he read aloud. '"Monopoly or Scrabble or some sort of board game as agreed upon. Tuesday night, cookery night."' He looked at her flushed, defiant face. '"Cookery night"? What the hell is *cookery night*?'

'Cookery night is an evening when you and Samantha prepare something together. It could be anything. A cake, perhaps, or some cookies. Or you could be even more adventurous and go for something hot. A casserole.'

'Cakes? Cookies? Casseroles?' His voice implied that she had asked him to fly to the moon and back. 'Isn't that *your* job?' he asked with heavy sarcasm. 'Correction. It shouldn't be a question. It's a statement of fact. Everything on this list consists of things *you* should be doing. In case you'd forgotten, my work keeps me out of the house for long periods of time.'

'I understand that you're a workaholic—'

'I'm not a workaholic.' He considered crumpling the list and chucking it into the bin, but was tempted to carry on reading. 'I run a company. Various companies. Believe it or not, it all takes time.'

'DVD night' was scheduled for Wednesday. He couldn't remember the last time he had watched a DVD. Who had time to sit in front of the television for hours on end? How productive was *that*?

'You have to make time for Samantha,' Tess told him stubbornly. 'I don't think you even know how scared she is of joining a new school. All her friends were at her school in Connecticut. She's terrified of making new ones!'

'Understandable, but kids adapt easily. It's a known fact.'

'That's easy for you to say,' Tess retorted, digging her heels in and refusing to budge. 'I can remember how scary it was going to secondary school! And I *knew* people who would be going with me. Just the thought of new teachers and new schoolbooks…'

'You didn't see it as a challenge you could rise to? No, maybe not, if you refused to settle down and do the work. But this isn't about you, and you're not Samantha. Granted, things haven't been easy for her, but being surrounded by new kids her own age will be a good thing. I'm *not*,' he said heavily, 'asking her to forget all the people she knew in Connecticut…'

'Maybe it feels that way to her.' Tess despaired of getting through to him. Where she had always seen the world in shades of grey, he seemed to see it entirely in black and white. Which, she wondered, was worse? The shades of grey that had prevented her from ever focusing on any one thing, or the black and white that seemed to prevent *him* from letting go of the reins for a second?

'What,' he asked, looking down at the list, 'is a "talking evening…"?'

'Ah. That one. I *was* going to slot in a games night…'

'I thought we had a Games night—where we play "Monopoly or Scrabble or some sort of other board game as agreed upon…"'

'I mean perhaps, take her to a rugby game. Maybe not rugby. Not in America, anyway. A soccer game. Or basketball. Or baseball. But then I really can't see you getting into any of that stuff.'

'Ah, *those* games. For guys who aren't workaholics…'

'You're not taking any of this seriously, are you?'

Matt looked at her speculatively. *Was* he taking any of it seriously? None of the previous nannies had presented him with lists before. He didn't think that any of them would have had the nerve. In fact he couldn't think, offhand, of anyone working for him who would have had the nerve to tell him what he should and shouldn't do.

On the other hand, none of the other nannies had had the success rate that she had—even after one day.

'Okay—here's the deal.' He sat back and folded his hands behind his head, the very picture of the dominant male. 'I'll consider some of your suggestions, but you'll have to be present.'

'Sorry?'

'Baking cookies and cakes… What do I know about that? My housekeeper looks after that side of things, or else I ensure food of the highest standard is delivered.'

'You just have to follow a recipe,' Tess pointed out. Did he even possess a recipe book? She hadn't seen any in the kitchen. Maybe he had a stash of them in his library—although she doubted that.

Matt stood up abruptly and walked towards the window, looking down at the matchstick figures scurrying along the pavements and the small yellow taxis like a toddler's play-cars.

'Have you shown this list to my daughter?' he asked, turning around to look at her.

In return she frowned at him. 'Not yet. I did it in the car on the way over. I mean, I *would* have had it typed out, but I…I didn't have time.'

'Then how do you know that she's going to go along with any of these schemes?'

'They're not *schemes*.'

'Okay. Ideas. Suggestions. Brainwaves. Call them what you want. How do you know that she's going to be keen to…let's say…play a board game for two hours?'

'Oh. Right. I see what you mean.'

'I very much doubt that,' Matt said irritably. 'Kids

these days prefer to sit in front of their computers. It's how they connect with their friends. Samantha has a very advanced computer. It was one of the first things I bought for her when she came here to live with me.'

'I'll do it,' Tess decided. 'If you need me around, then I'll do it.'

Need was a word that didn't feature heavily in his vocabulary—not insofar as it applied to him, at any rate. He opened his mouth to point that out, and then realised that, like it or not, the prospect of trying to coax a positive reaction from his daughter whilst trying to appear relaxed in front of a game of Scrabble was the equivalent of looking up at an insurmountable precipice and trying to work out how to scale it in a pair of flip-flops.

'It's hardly a question of need,' he stated, frowning.

'Some men find it difficult to take time out for quality family time…'

'Spare me the psychobabble, Tess.'

He met her eyes and for a split second she felt almost dizzy. She wondered whether it was because she was just so unused to any of this. Standing up for something and refusing to back down. Telling a man like Matt Strickland—who was her sister's *boss*, for goodness' sake—that he *should* be doing stuff, when it was obvious that no one *ever* told him what he should be doing. Getting involved enough to go beyond the call of duty for a job she had been reluctant to accept in the first place.

Her mouth went dry and she found that she was sitting on her hands, leaning forward in her chair. Crazy!

'It's not psychobabble,' she said faintly. 'It's the

truth! What activity would you…would you like to start with?'

'Ah. A choice?' Matt looked at the list. 'You do realise that choosing to participate in these activities will curtail your free time in the evenings?'

'That's okay.'

'I'll make sure that you're paid overtime, of course.'

'I don't care about the money,' Tess muttered, looking in fascination at his downbent head as he continued to frown over the list, as though trying to work out which was the most acceptable of the options on the table.

'But you might,' he murmured, not looking at her, 'regret committing to something that's going to involve time you might otherwise spend seeing New York…going out and having fun. Isn't that going to be a problem?'

Quite suddenly he raised his eyes to hers, and there it was again—that giddy feeling as though she was free-falling through space.

'Why should it be a problem?' she asked breathlessly.

'Because,' Matt murmured, 'you're young, and I've gathered that you came here to have fun. Since when has your definition of *fun* been spending time with your employer and his daughter, playing a game of Scrabble?'

Never, Tess thought, confused.

'Right.' He stood up, and she hastily followed suit. Her allotted time was over. 'First of all, you will be reimbursed—whether you like it or not. And as for which activity takes my fancy…having done none of them for longer than I can remember…'

He grinned. A smile of genuine amusement. And

for a few heart-stopping seconds he ceased to be Matt Strickland, the man who was employing her, the man who represented just the sort of staid workaholic that she privately abhorred, and was just a man. A suffocatingly sexy man who made her head spin.

'Your choice. I'll be home tomorrow by six.'

CHAPTER THREE

'OKAY. So let me get this straight. You've now got yourself a clothes allowance, no limits, and *you're going on a date with my boss*.'

'It's not a date,' Tess said irritably, but she was only half concentrating on Claire who was lounging fully clothed in a tight green dress with high heels—also green. Claire was killing time before going out with the guy she had been seeing for the past eighteen months—an investment banker whom Tess had met several times and liked very much, despite the fact that the second he left the room she could never seem to quite remember what he looked like.

'No? What is it, then? Cosy restaurant? Bottle of Chablis? Candlelight? No one's ever had a clue as to what Matt Strickland does in his private life, and here you are, less than three weeks in, and *you're on a date*.'

Small and black or small and red? Tess was thinking, looking at the selection of outfits she had bought earlier that day. Five seconds of tussling with her moral conscience and she had shamelessly capitulated once inside the fashionable department store to which she had been directed—because, he had told her, he would be taking her to dinner to get her feedback, and she would need something fairly dressy to wear. Were it not for him, she'd reasoned to herself, she wouldn't have to spend money on clothes for restaurants she wouldn't be going to. So if he wanted to foot the bill, then why not?

Besides, Samantha had been having fun. They had made a deal. Tess would pretend to yawn inside the toy shops and Samantha would tap the over-sized face of her newly acquired Disney watch in boredom inside the grown-up clothes shops, and then they would break for lunch at a place upon which they had both agreed, and which was based on a menu of pizzas and burgers. Good, fortifying food before they dutifully visited some place of culture in the name of education.

Tess had discovered that in New York there was a cultural destination for every day of the week for at least a year. Having always considered places of culture as unutterably boring, she was slowly discovering that they weren't half bad—especially when being explored with someone with an equal lack of knowledge. Even if that particular someone happened to be a ten-and-nine tenths-of-a-year-old child. They would learn together along the way, and it had to be said that Samantha was as sharp as a tack. Indeed, Tess had delegated most of the guidebooks to her, and her job was to describe what they were looking at, including its history.

'I think I'll go red.'

'Why do you care if it's not a date?' Claire smirked, easing herself off the bed and dusting herself down. 'And please don't tell me again that it's not a date. For the past three weeks I've hardly seen you, and now you're off to a restaurant with him. Surely you've said everything there is to say over your games of Monopoly and your cinema evenings?'

'Has it been three weeks?' Yes. Yes, it had. Time seemed to be moving at the speed of sound. After her initial hesitation about getting involved with Matt and the tense relationship he had with his daughter, she seemed to have dived in—headlong. Games night—their first night—had been a muted success, and since then things had picked up because he had been making an effort. He was getting back to the apartment before seven without fail, and throwing himself into every activity with such enthusiasm that it was difficult not to be swept away along with him. Samantha, wary at first, was slowly beginning to thaw, beginning to really enjoy herself, and it was hard not to be caught up in the changing tide.

'It's a *debriefing*,' Tess concluded. 'And I only wish I didn't have to go. I'd much rather be living it up in Manhattan on a Friday night out with you and Tom. Okay, maybe not you and Tom, but with other people. Young, exciting people. Artists and writers and poets.' The sort of people she thought she *should* be thrilled to hang out with, in other words. 'I haven't really had a chance to report back to Matt on how things are going with Samantha. This is purely about my job. I think I've put on weight. Have I put on weight? This dress feels a bit snug.'

'Tess…' Claire said hesitantly. 'You're not going to do anything stupid, are you?'

'Anything stupid? Like what?'

'I don't know what Matt Strickland gets up to in his

personal life, but there's a reason why he is where he is today. He's tough and he's pretty ruthless…'

'What are you trying to say?'

'Don't fall for the guy.'

'I wouldn't!' Tess turned to her sister. 'My dream guy isn't a high-flier who wants to make money. You know that. My dream guy is down to earth and sensitive, and when I find him I'll recognise him.'

'That's not how life works.'

'I'm just doing my job, and for the first time in my life I'm actually enjoying what I'm doing. You have no idea what it's like to see Matt and Samantha together. Okay, it's not perfect, but it's beginning to work, and I'd like to think that I've had something to do with that. It seems to me that the whole world wants me to settle down and find something I wants to stick with. I think I've found it. I like children and I like working with them. It's something positive that I'm going to take away from this whole experience and please don't confuse that with anything else!'

It was the first time she had come even close to being at odds with her sister, and she relented as soon as she saw Claire's shocked expression.

'I can take care of myself, so don't worry about me. I'm not falling for Matt Strickland! I'm getting to know him. And the only reason I'm getting to know him is because I need to for the sake of his daughter.'

She could have added that Matt Strickland had become three-dimensional, and that her head was slowly becoming crowded with images of him. Matt frowning in concentration in front of a recipe book for beginners she and Samantha had bought three days ago. Matt exultant when he managed to buy a hotel and charge exorbitant rent in a game of Monopoly. Matt teasing but tentative as his daughter brought him hesitantly into her life in Connecticut over the images of her friends on her computer.

This dinner, she knew, was purely about business. He would point out any areas of concern he had with her. He would see room for improvement. No need for nerves, and no need to be unsettled by anything Claire had said.

For the first time Tess was beginning to get a handle on just how much she had been protected through the years by her parents and by her sisters. They had allowed her to retreat from the competitive race academically. Claire and Mary had indulged her when she had turned her back on schoolwork. Had they felt sorry for her because they'd known how impossible it would be to live up to the standards they had set? Or had they enjoyed vicariously living a different kind of life through her? A life without responsibilities? And her parents had been almost as bad. No wonder Claire now thought that she was incapable of protecting herself when it came to the big, bad world! The fact was that she was finally growing up. She was taking on responsibilities. She was more equipped now that she had ever been to deal with whatever life threw at her.

Self-confidence restored, she slipped on the red dress, stuck on high, wedge-heeled sandals with delicate straps, and then stood back and examined her reflection in the mirror.

She didn't often do this—stare critically at herself in the mirror—but doing it now, really taking time to see how she looked, she wasn't disappointed. She would never be tall and spindly, but she looked okay. Her hair was loose and it shone, and she was already acquiring a healthy glow from the baking summer sun. Claire and Mary both had a typically Irish complexion: dark hair, pale skin with a hint of freckles, and of course the family trademark—bright green eyes. Tess, however, was warmer in colour, and it showed. The sun had also lightened her hair. She wasn't blonde, but lighter, with more varied shades of caramel.

With Claire loitering somewhere outside, ready to resume their conversation, Tess waited until Matt's driver paged her on her cell phone and then hurried out of the apartment, stopping to peep into the kitchen only to announce that she was off.

After three weeks she had become accustomed to being driven around New York. She no longer felt like royalty inside the limo, and she was hardly aware of the streets slipping by until the car finally stopped outside an elegant restaurant—just the sort of restaurant that would have chucked her out had she turned up in her normal gear of jeans and a tee shirt.

Stanton, Matt's driver, swooped round to open the car door for her.

Inside, a small foyer opened to an expanse of gleaming wooden floors and circular tables with starched white linen tablecloths and comfortable brown leather chairs. Every table seemed to be full of people chattering and, frankly, looking unashamedly glamorous. It was almost as though a Hollywood director had decided to film a movie inside a restaurant and supplied his own cast.

Two impressive wooden tables were home to the most towering vases of flowers Tess had ever seen. White lilies intricately laced around a honeycomb of twisted driftwood neatly partitioned the restaurant, so that there was at once an atmosphere of pleasant busyness that was yet strangely intimate.

Even by the impossibly high standards of opulence to which she had been exposed, this was in a league of its own, and Matt, sipping a drink and waiting for her in the most private corner of the restaurant, looked perfectly at ease in the surroundings.

Nervous tension beaded her upper lip, and suddenly, unexpectedly, her body was doing strange things. For a few seconds her breathing seemed to stop, and—perversely—her heart began beating so fast that it felt as though it would burst out of her chest. Her mind had shut down. There was not a thought in her head. Even the sound of the diners and the clatter of cutlery faded to a background blur.

He was wearing a black jacket that fitted him like a glove, and the white of his shirt threw the aristocratic harsh angles of his face into stunning prominence. He looked vibrant and drop-dead gorgeous, and she almost faltered in her high heels as she walked towards him.

In the act of lifting his glass to his lips, he seemed to still too.

Suddenly self-conscious, and embarrassed at being caught red-handed in the act of staring, Tess plastered a brilliant smile on her lips as she weaved her way towards him.

'I didn't realise that we would be having a meeting in such grand surroundings,' she carolled gaily, making sure to get the conversation onto neutral work-orientated territory as soon as possible. If nothing else, it did wonders to distract her from the glimpse of hard-muscled chest just visible where the top two buttons of his shirt were undone, and the way his fine dark hair curled alluringly around the dull silver strap of his watch.

Matt tore his eyes away from her and glanced round at the sumptuous décor which he casually took for granted. 'The food's good. It's the reason I keep coming back here. French food always makes a change from steak.'

'Not nearly as good as the spaghetti Bolognese your daughter cooked for you a few days ago, though. You have no idea how long it took us to stockpile all the ingredients. Everything had to be just right. The mushrooms. The shallots. The quality of the mince.'

Tess was babbling. Where had this sudden attack of nerves come from, she wondered. She had seen enough of Matt Strickland in the past few weeks to have killed any nerves she might have around him, surely? But her pulses were still racing and her mouth still felt dry, even after the two hefty sips of wine she'd gulped down from the crystal wine glass in front of her.

'And let's not go into the length of time it took us to find just the right recipe book,' she confided. 'I think Samantha looked at every single one at three separate bookshops. I had to stop her from trying to wheedle me into buying her a pasta machine. Can you believe it? I told her that it might be better to start simple and then move on to the complicated stuff. You…er…have an incredibly well-equipped kitchen. Everything new and shiny…' She trailed off in the face of his unnerving silence. 'Why aren't you saying anything?' she asked awkwardly. 'I thought you wanted me here to talk about how things were coming along with Samantha.'

'You have a way of running away with the conversation,' Matt murmured. 'It's always interesting to see where it's going to lead.'

Tess tried and failed to take that as a compliment. The smile she directed at him was a little wobbly at the edges. 'You make me sound like a kid,' she said in a forced voice, and he tilted his head to one side, as though giving that observation some thought.

'Maybe that's why you've worked out so well as her nanny.' He flashed her a veiled amused look, but for some reason Tess was finding it hard to see the funny side. 'The other nannies the agency supplied were nothing like you. They were far more regimented. Samantha refused to be told what to do, ran circles around them, and they eventually ended up handing in their notice. The more she had, the more I gave instructions to the agency that the next one should be stricter. I can see now that it was completely the wrong ploy. I should have been trying to find someone who was more on her level.'

'How many did she have?'

'Five—although one only lasted three days. They did their best to discipline her. In nine times out of ten they might have had success with that approach…'

'*I* discipline her,' Tess interrupted defensively.

'Do you? How?'

'If you don't like the way I do things…'

'Don't be ridiculous, Tess. Haven't I just told you how well I think you're doing? You've achieved wonders in a matter of weeks!'

'But I don't want you to think that the only reason

I've succeeded is because I let her do exactly what she wants! You gave me permission to get her a new wardrobe of clothes. Do you remember I discussed this with you? Do you remember I told you to look around at the other kids her age in New York and see what they were wearing? When she goes to her new school she might find it easier if she shows up in the same sort of clothes as everyone else. I said all this to you and you agreed! So we went shopping and, yes, some of her things *did* come from markets, but she'd never been to a market before. She enjoyed the experience!'

'How have we landed up here?'

'We've landed up here because…because…' What should have been a cool, businesslike conversation in relaxed surroundings was falling apart at the seams—and it was *her* fault. Was it any wonder that he was staring at her as though she had taken leave of her senses? He had complimented her on her progress and she had responded by snapping. She was miserably aware that she had snapped because she didn't want him implying that she was somehow immature, and she wasn't sure why she cared.

'Because it hasn't all been about Samantha having fun. I've had to really coax her out of her shell, and I admit it's easier to coax a child when you dangle something in front of her that she wants. But I've also been doing schoolwork with her…'

'Yes. I know.'

'You do?'

'She's told me.'

Tess didn't miss the flash of quiet satisfaction that crossed his face, and she made a big effort to remind herself that *this* was why she so enjoyed the job. Because she had been instrumental in helping to heal some of the rifts between Matt and his daughter. And if Matt patted her on the back and patronisingly complimented her on getting the job done because she was immature enough to win over her charge, then so be it.

'You've proved yourself wrong.' He leaned back in the chair as menus were placed in front of them and more wine was poured into glasses. 'How does that feel?'

'I've only gone through the basic stuff with her,' Tess mumbled, blushing.

'It's a mountain when your starting point was insisting that you were incapable of doing simple maths and science.'

A slow, palpable sense of pleasure radiated through her, made her feel hot and flustered, and although she knew that his dark, lazy eyes were on her, she couldn't bring herself to meet them.

'Well, I won't be taking a degree course in them any time soon.' Tess laughed breathlessly.

Claire might have given her long lectures about his ruthlessness, but this was a side of him to which she had been not privy. Claire hadn't seen the complete human being. She had just seen the guy who issued orders and expected obedience.

'But doing something of which you didn't think yourself capable must have gone some distance to bolstering your self-confidence…'

Her eyes flew to his, and she had a few giddy seconds of imagining that those dark, deep, brooding eyes of his could see right down to the very heart of her. Her voice was shaky as she gave her order to the waiter, and when she thought that the conversation might move on she was greeted with a mildly expectant silence.

'I've always had bags of self-confidence,' she muttered eventually. 'You can ask either of my sisters. While they were buried under heaps of books, I was always out having a great time with my friends.' Why did she get the feeling that he didn't believe her? And his disbelief had to be infectious, because she was almost failing to believe herself. 'I may not be going out a great deal in the evenings now, because of my working hours,' she said, relentlessly pursuing the point even though he hadn't contradicted a word she had said, 'but I'm normally the kind of girl who always had lots of invitations.'

'And you miss that?'

'We're not here to talk about me.'

'But in a way we are,' Matt pointed out smoothly. 'You spend more time with my daughter than I do. It's important for me to know your frame of mind. I wouldn't want to think that you might be storing up resentments. So...you've spent most of your evenings over the past few weeks at my apartment. Does that bother you? When you're accustomed to spending your time going out with friends?'

He watched her fiddle with the stem of her wine glass. Her cheeks were flushed. Her thick, straight, toffee-coloured hair hung like a silky curtain over her shoulders, halfway down her back. Amidst the plush, formal surroundings she looked very, very young, and suddenly he felt very, very old. A quick glance around him confirmed that there was almost no one in the restaurant under the age of fifty. The fabulously high prices excluded all but the very rich, and he was an exception when it came to being very rich and the right side of forty. He had grown up in an ivory tower and had never had cause to leave it. It discomfited him to think that curiosity, if nothing else, should have driven him out at least for a brief period of time.

Annoyed to find himself succumbing, even temporarily, to an unusual bout of passing introspection, Matt frowned, and Tess, seeing the change of expression, was instantly on her guard.

Was he going to tell her that she needed to stop spending her evenings at his home? Did he *disapprove*? Maybe he hankered after more one-to-one time with Samantha and she, blithely unconcerned, was in the process of just *getting in the way.*

Maybe she should suggest reverting to normal working hours…

Dismayed, Tess realised that she didn't want to do that. How had that happened? How had Matt Strickland and his daughter and their complicated family life suddenly become so integral to her day-to-day existence?

Her thoughts were in a whirl as food was placed in front of them—exquisite arrangements of shellfish and potatoes that Tess would have dived into with gusto were it not for the feverish whirring of her mind.

'I'll curtail my hours if you want me to,' she heard herself say in a small voice.

'I don't believe that's what I was asking you,' Matt told her impatiently. He had become accustomed to her never ending cheerfulness, and the despondent droop of her shoulders made him feel like the Grinch who stole

Christmas. 'You're my employee,' he said tightly. 'And I have certain obligations as your employer.'

Tess hated that professional appraisal. She realised that she didn't *want* him to have any obligations as the guy who had hired her, but when she started to think about what she *did* want her thoughts did that crazy thing again and became tangled and confusing.

'I wouldn't want you to turn around at some later date and accuse me of taking advantage of you.'

'I would never do that!' Tess was horrified and offended.

'You've insisted on forgoing any overtime payments…'

'You pay me enough as it is! I *like* sticking around in the evenings and helping out with Samantha.'

'Doesn't do much good for a social life for you, though, does it?'

'I didn't come over here to cultivate a social life,' Tess said firmly. Well, she admitted to herself, that *was* a bit of an exaggeration, thinking back to the dismay with which she had greeted the suggestion of a job, but that was in the past so it didn't count. 'I came here to try and get my act together and I have.' Her natural warmth was returning and she smiled at him. 'I feel like I've finally found something I really enjoy doing. I mean, I think I have an affinity with kids. I don't get bored with them. You'd be surprised how clever and insightful Samantha can be without even realising it. I can get all the socialising that I want when I get back home.' Which was something she wasn't going to start thinking about just yet.

'And do you socialise with anyone in particular there?'

'What do you mean?'

'You're an attractive young woman.' Matt shrugged and pushed aside his plate, which was swept up by a waiter seconds later. 'Left any broken hearts behind?'

'Oh, hundreds!' Tess said gaily. If he thought that she was immature and green around the ears, how much more cemented would that impression be if he knew that being 'one of the lads' and having loads of friends who happened to be boys was a far cry from having a solid relationship with one in particular.

'So was that part of the reason you came over here?'

'No!' Tess protested uncomfortably.

'Because no boy is worth it. Not at your age.'

'I'm twenty-three. Not thirteen.' Just in case he had missed that, which she suspected he had. Because she had never, not once, caught him looking at her with male interest. While she…Tess flushed and felt something scary and powerful stir in her, as though finally being allowed to take shape. *She* had looked at *him*. Released from their Pandora's Box, little snapshots of him began swirling in her head. The way he looked when he was laughing, the way he raised his eyebrows in lazy amusement, that half-smile that could send shivers down her spine—except it hadn't. Not until now.

Uncomfortable in her own skin, Tess struggled to get her thoughts in order while her innocuous remark hovered in the air between them, challenging him to assess her in a different way altogether.

As though the reins of his rigid self-control had

suddenly been snapped, Matt was assailed by a series of powerful, destabilising images. She might look young, with the stunning attraction of dewy skin and an open, expressive face that was a rare commodity in the hard-bitten world in which he lived, but she wasn't thirteen. She especially didn't look like a teenager in that dress she was wearing, which left just enough to get the imagination doing all sorts of interesting things. It took massive will-power to pull himself back from the brink of plunging headlong into the tempting notion of taking her to his bed.

She was his daughter's nanny! What the hell was going on in his head? It grated on him to know that this wasn't the first time he had played with the idea. He should know better. Work and play mixed as successfully as oil and water. He had never brought his private life to work and he wasn't about to start now. Tess Kelly might not hold down a job within the physical walls of his offices, but she was as much his employee as any one of the hundreds who worked for him.

And, even taking that small but vital technicality out of the equation, Tess Kelly didn't conform to anything he required from a woman. Having lived through the horror that had been his marriage, wedded in unhappy matrimony to a woman who had fulfilled all the requirements on paper and none in practice, as it turned out, his checklist when it came to women was stringent.

It was essential that they were as focused as he was. Focused and independent, with careers that were demanding enough to stave off any need for them to rely on him to define their lives. Like him, Catrina had come from old money, and her life had consisted of fundraisers and charity balls and lunches and all those other little things that had left her with plenty of time to decide that his duty was to provide a never-ending diet of excitement. There had been no need for her to work, and she had, in any case, never been programmed for it. And into the void of all those empty hours when he had been working had crept the seeds of bitterness and disenchantment. She had wanted a rich partner who wanted to play, and he had failed to fulfil the specification. In the aftermath of that experience, and the consequences it came to entail, Matt was diligent in never straying beyond his own self-imposed boundaries.

Belatedly, because she had been away and contact between them had been sporadic and via e-mail, he remembered Vicky. She was in Hong Kong, getting a taste for the Eastern markets. She was due back in a couple of days' time. He tried to pull up a memory of what she looked like, but the second he thought of her dark tailored bob and the neat precision of her personality another image of a bubbly, golden-haired girl with a dusting of freckles on her nose and a personality that was all over the place superimposed itself on the woman who claimed to be dying to catch up with him.

Irritated, he frowned. Then his face cleared and that vague feeling of being out of sorts began to ebb away.

'Tell me your plans for the next few days.' He pushed himself away from the table and signalled to the waiter for some coffees.

'Plans?' Still fretting over her tumultuous thoughts, it took Tess a few seconds to register that he had completely changed the subject. 'A museum, and then a quiet day just relaxing with Samantha tomorrow. Maybe I'll grab an early evening and catch up with my social life, now that you've put that idea into my head.'

'And then on Friday perhaps we might visit the zoo…' said Matt.

This was a breakthrough. Instead of just following the tide, he was actually generating an idea of his own! Pure delight was all over her face as she nodded approvingly. She would take a back seat, watch father and daughter together, remind herself that her involvement with them both began and ended as a job.

And Matt, watching her carefully from under lowered lashes, calculated on Vicky's presence. The two of them, side by side, would squash uninvited rebellious thoughts for which he had no use. He and Vicky might not be destined for the long haul, but she would be a timely reminder of what he was looking for in the opposite sex.

Matters sorted satisfactorily, and feeling back in control, he signalled for the bill.

CHAPTER FOUR

OVER the next two days Tess had ample opportunity to think about herself. Matt had asked some very relevant questions, and had kick-started a chain of thoughts that made her uneasily aware that the things about herself she had always taken for granted might just be built on a certain amount of delusion.

She had always considered herself a free spirit. Her sisters had been the unfortunate recipients of their parents' ambitions. Neither of their parents had gone to university. Their mother had worked as a dinner lady at the local school, and their father had held down a job in the accounts department at an electrical company. But, they were both really clever, and in another time and another place would have gone to university and fulfilled all sorts of dreams. They hadn't, though, and consequently had taken an inordinate interest and delight in Claire and Mary's superhuman academic achievements.

Tess had set her own agenda from an early age and had never deviated. Just in case her parents got it into their heads that she was destined to follow the same path, she had firmly set her own benchmark.

She had always thought that she loved *living* too much to waste time hiding away in a room in front of a pile of books. She liked *sampling* things, getting a taste for different experiences. She refused to be tied down and she had always been proud of her thirst for freedom.

Matt's take on things had badly damaged that glib acceptance. She wondered whether her happy-go-lucky attitude stemmed from a deep-rooted fear of competition. If you didn't try, then you weren't going to fail—as he had said to her on day one—and she had never tried and so had never set herself up for a fall. She had been offended and resentful at his implication that she lacked self-confidence, and yet she knew that she had never made the most of her talents. Underneath the pretty, popular, happy-go-lucky girl, had there always been an anxious, scared one, covering up her insecurities by wanting to be seen as the antidote to her sisters? Had she cultivated her social life—always being there for other people, always willing to lend a hand and always in demand—because that had helped her prove to herself that she was every bit as valuable as her two clever sisters?

Tess didn't like this train of thought, but, having started, she was finding it impossible to stop. One thought seemed to generate another. It was as though a locked door had suddenly been flung open and out had spilled all manner of lost, forgotten and deliberately misplaced things from her childhood.

For the first time she had no inclination to share her thoughts with her sister, indeed, was relieved that Claire had taken herself off for a week's break with Tom and wouldn't be returning until the middle of the following week.

As she was getting ready on Friday morning for their

expedition to the zoo, Tess made herself address the other discomforting issue that had been nagging the back of her mind—the other loaded pistol that Matt had pointed at her head and forced her to acknowledge. *Why* had she suddenly jettisoned her social life? Why? She had arrived in Manhattan a carefree, fun-loving girl, with no thoughts beyond enjoying a lovely break from Ireland and perhaps trying to figure out what job to apply for when she returned. So how had she suddenly found herself in the position of willingly sacrificing her social life for the sake of a job? Why did the thought of going out and having a good time with young people her own age leave her cold? Of course she enjoyed Samantha, and loved the small changes in her personality she could detect as the days passed. It was rewarding to watch the person emerge from the protective, wary shell—like watching a butterfly emerge from its cocoon—but beyond that she just really liked being in Matt's company because she fancied him.

Tess hadn't recognised that for what it was because she didn't think she had ever truly fancied anyone before. She had never questioned all those stolen glances and the way her body responded when he was around. Even now, as she wriggled into a navy and white striped vest and brushed out her hair before tying it up into a ponytail, she could feel her body tingling at the thought of seeing him. *That* was why she had thought nothing of putting her social life on hold. *That* was why she was happy to spend evenings at his apartment, sometimes just sitting cross-legged on the sofa with Samantha, watching something on the telly, while on the chair close by Matt pretended to watch with the newspaper in front of him and a drink at his side.

Tess felt a little thrill of excitement race through her. She was in lust, and it felt good even if nothing would come of it. Because she certainly hadn't caught him stealing any glances at *her*, and she couldn't imagine him thinking about her in some way—not the way she realised she thought about him.

Tess could only assume that the very sheltered life she had led was the reason why she was only now feeling things that most women her age would have felt long ago. Where her sisters had flown the nest and pursued university degrees, then moved to new, exciting cities to begin their illustrious careers, she had remained at home, circulating with more or less the same crowd she had grown up with—a protective little circle that had, she could see now, been comforting and restrictive in equal measure. She felt as though she was finally emerging from cold storage. It was exciting. And who knew what lay round the corner? she thought, with the optimism with which she had always greeted most situations.

The journey to Pelham Parkway was baking hot, but she had dressed for the heat in a pair of cool linen trousers and flip-flops. It was going to be a long day. The zoo was enormous—one of the largest urban zoos. She had agreed with Matt that she would contact him by text as soon as she arrived, so that they could agree a meeting point, but with this new awareness of him burning a hole in her she found herself texting Samantha instead, and then making her way to a convenient spot where she could wait for them to finish their animal sightseeing on the monorail.

On the way, her stomach rumbling, she bought herself a giant hot dog, and was sinking her teeth gratefully into the eight-inch sausage, onion, ketchup and mustard indulgence when she spotted Samantha running towards her.

Samantha was no longer the primly dressed ten-year-old of a few weeks ago. She was in a pair of trendy cut-off denims, some flat espadrilles and a tee shirt that advertised a teenage musical.

'Have a bite.' Tess offered the hot dog to her and stood up. 'I'm never going to finish this.' She was driven to search out Matt, but resisted the impulse.

'I thought you were giving up junk food.' Samantha took the hot dog and smiled up at her. 'Because you were piling on the pounds.'

'Next Monday. I have it pencilled in my diary.'

'Anyway, they're waiting for us, so we'd better go.'

'They…?'

'Vicky was tired and had to rest, even though she's been sitting on the monorail for twenty minutes.' Samantha made a face while Tess confusedly tried to compute a name that meant nothing to her and had never been mentioned before. Was Vicky a relative?

She hurried after Samantha, and after a few minutes came to a shuddering halt by a café—one of the many that were dotted around the zoo. It was packed. Kids were eating ice cream, infants with more common sense than the adults were howling in pushchairs because they were hot and sticky and wanted to leave. She could easily have missed the couple sitting at the back, because they were surrounded by families trying to find somewhere to sit and children being called back to tables by anxious parents. But her eyes were automatically drawn to Matt and she grinned, because he looked just as she would have expected him to look away from the comforts to which he was accustomed. He was a man who took for granted the bliss of air-conditioning in summer and the luxury of personal shoppers who did everything for him and spared him the inconvenience of having to do battle with crowds. It was a real indication of how determined he was to involve himself with his daughter that he would ever have suggested a zoo expedition and accepted this less than luxurious experience as a necessary consequence.

For a few seconds she found it hard to tear her eyes away from him. In a pair of light tan trousers and a navy blue polo shirt, he looked dark and sexy and dangerous. He was wearing dark sunglasses, which he proceeded to remove, and the thought of his eyes on her as she tried to manoeuvre a path through the crowds sent a little shiver down her spine.

She could fully understand how he had managed to turn her notion of sexual attraction on its head. She had foolishly assumed that because he represented the sort of man she didn't find attractive personality wise her body would just fall in line and likewise fail to respond. She hadn't bargained on the fact that her body would have a will of its own and would go haring off in the opposite direction.

Samantha had made it to him, and it was only when they were both looking at her that Tess took in the woman sitting next to him at the small, circular metal table. For a few seconds her steps faltered, because if this was a relative then she certainly wasn't a relative of the comfortable variety.

Holding a cup primly between her fingers, and with dark shades concealing all expression, was a strikingly attractive woman with an expertly tailored bob that was sharply cut to chin level. A pale lemon silk cardigan was casually draped over her shoulders.

Matt half stood as she reached the table but his companion remained seated, although she pushed the shades onto her head revealing cool brown eyes.

'Tess…I'd like you to meet Vicky.'

The expected return of his common sense was failing to materialise. It had been a trying morning. Samantha had been disappointed that their cosy party of three had expanded to include Vicky, and although Matt told himself that it was healthy for her to deal with the fact that Tess was not a member of the family he had still felt as though some of the progress he had made with his daughter had been somehow undermined by the inclusion of Vicky in their day out.

And then had come his disappointing reaction to seeing Vicky. His interest had not been re-ignited, and indeed he had been irritated by her.

She had had precious little contact with Samantha before her three week visit to Hong Kong, but had immediately seen fit to try and establish a relationship. He had been all too aware that his daughter had retreated into herself and had blamed him for this unwelcome development.

All in all, a bit of a nightmare, and now, seeing Tess

next to Vicky, he was already beginning to draw unwelcome comparisons.

'You're the nanny!' Vicky offered a cool smile. 'Matt's told me about you in his e-mails. What a blessing that you turned up when you did! This little thing has been super-naughty with her nannies—haven't you, sweetie? You're very young, aren't you?'

E-mails? Tess didn't like the thought of being discussed behind her back, and it was dawning on her that this was Matt's girlfriend. The fact that he even had one came as a shock, but as the reality of it began to sink in she wondered how on earth she could ever have expected otherwise. Men like Matt Stickland were never short of women throwing themselves at him. He was as rich as Croesus and sinfully good-looking. Now, in light of this, her silly infatuation with him—if it could even be called that—struck her as tellingly naïve.

This woman was far more the type he would go for, even if his body language was saying otherwise. She was clever and accomplished, and, as the day progressed, Tess was left in very little doubt that there was absolutely nothing the woman hadn't already achieved or else was about to.

Vicky talked non-stop. She tried to make jokes with Matt, who smiled stiffly and contributed very little to the conversation. She gave long, educational lectures to Samantha about every animal they passed and was undeterred by the silent, faintly hostile response. She confided in Tess every qualification she had ever gained and her progress in her career step by step, starting with when she was a lowly junior manager and culminating in her exalted position now, as CEO of one of the largest listed companies in America. She was smart and she was self-confident, and she had scaled heights in her career that most women might only ever dream of.

Matt wouldn't raise his eyebrows and make some dry, amused remark about *her* taste in television programmes. He would have informed discussions with her and talk about everything from the state of the economy to world politics.

Tess waited two and a half hours before she felt it polite to tell them that she would be on her way. Samantha, like her, was drooping, and had been for a while. A small, quiet bundle, shorn of the tentative beginnings of exuberance that had marked the past week or so.

What a hellish disaster, Matt thought in raging frustration. What the *hell* was Vicky's agenda? She had monopolised the conversation, glorified herself, done her level best to ingratiate herself with Samantha.

'You've hardly been here two minutes.' He frowned at Tess, who was fidgeting apologetically, playing with the clasp on the leather satchel slung over her shoulder. 'What do you mean *you're going*?'

'I have some stuff to do.'

'Your working day hasn't come to an end. It's not yet five-thirty.'

He felt, with considerable irritation, Vicky's arm link through his and the weight of her as she leant against him.

'We could go off and do something,' Samantha interjected in a cool, childish voice. 'Tess could drop me home. Couldn't you, Tess? We could even stop off and have something to eat on the way. Burgers and fries,' she added, because somewhere along the line there had been a long lecture from Vicky on the dangers of the wrong diet. At the time she had been focusing on the last of the hot dog disappearing into Samantha's mouth.

'You'll leave with us,' Matt rasped, sliding his eyes down to where his daughter was staring at him, sullen and tight-lipped. 'And I don't want any arguments, Samantha. I'm your father and you'll do as I say.'

In the sweltering heat, tempers were frayed. Tess miserably wondered whether Matt would rather have stayed at home with his girlfriend. Did his foul mood stem from the fact that he could think of better things to be doing with his time? Didn't he know that his relationship with Samantha was still so fragile that coming down heavy on her now was going to jeopardise everything they had begun building together?

She felt as though she had failed them both. She told herself stoutly that their relationship wasn't her concern, that she was just a ship in the night, passing through their lives, but right here, with people bustling around them and Samantha looking to be on the verge of tears, Tess suddenly felt miserable and depressed.

'I'll be at work bright and early on Monday morning,' Tess said brightly. 'Or we could even do something tomorrow, if you like...?' This was to Samantha, but Vicky was quick to step in, smiling and giving Matt's arm a gentle squeeze.

'We'll be fine.' Her voice was hard as nails. 'I just got back from the Far East. I'd quite like to have my little unit to myself over the weekend. Besides, don't you have anything better to do than spend your Saturday with a ten-year-old child?'

Those ringing words were a timely reminder to Tess that she needed to get her act together. Hadn't Matt mentioned something along those lines to her himself? Had he and his girlfriend been exchanging jokey e-mails about her? The sad little nanny with no life to speak of in one of the most exciting cities in the world?

The journey back to her sister's apartment was long and hot and tedious. The upside was that there would be no one around to question her tearful mood. The downside was that she did, actually, feel as though she needed a sympathetic shoulder to cry on.

Nothing could distract her from the sobering realisation that she had made a complete fool of herself by lusting after a man who wasn't interested in her. It was a sign of her own vanity—which was something she had never even known she *possessed*—that she hadn't once stopped to ask herself whether he was involved with a woman. There had seemed to be none on the scene, and he had mentioned no names, and so she had made her own incorrect conclusions.

It was a little after eight when the buzzer sounded. Claire had an intercom system in her flat. It was an excellent way of avoiding unwanted visitors. You could see them on the little television-style screen and then just duck low until they got the message and disappeared.

Her heart flipped when she made out Matt's face. He looked impatient and at the end of his tether, and she was determined to ignore him, but instead found herself picking up the phone to ask him what he wanted.

'You. I need to talk to you.'

'What about? I thought you were going to be spending

the weekend playing house with your girlfriend.' She clapped her hand to her mouth. 'I'm sorry I said that. I'm tired. Can it wait until Monday?'

'No. It can't. Buzz me up.'

'What's so important?' Tess persisted. 'I'm about ready to go to bed.'

'It's not even nine. It's a Friday evening. You're not ready to go to bed. Buzz me up.'

'What do you want!' was the first thing she asked when he was standing in the doorway, filling it out and sending her nervous system into frantic disarray. He was still in the clothes he had worn to the zoo. She, however, had changed, and was now wearing a pair of black pyjama bottoms and a small vest. No bra. She folded her arms and backed away, following him with her eyes as he strode into the apartment and headed directly to the kitchen.

'I think,' he said, opening the fridge and extracting a bottle of beer, which he proceeded to flick open after he had hunted down a bottle opener in one of the drawers, 'I need a drink.'

'Look, you can't just barge in here—'

'Your sister's away, isn't she? Visiting the boyfriend's parents, if I remember correctly?'

'Who is with Samantha? Is…is your girlfriend with her?'

Matt drained a quarter of the bottle in one long, thirsty gulp while looking at her as she hovered to the side, ill at ease and wary. Tension was climbing its way up her spine. What did he want? When she thought about the excitement that had infused her at the start of the day, when she had dressed with thoughts of him in her head, she felt humiliation washing over her all over again.

'Today didn't go as planned.' Matt finished the beer, wondered whether to have another. But he had already drunk too much for his own good—had had to get his driver to ferry him across to Tess's apartment. Hell, what else was alcohol for, if not to smooth away the rough edges of uncomfortable situations? He had made an appalling mistake in asking Vicky to accompany them. It had been a massive error of judgement. And for a man who could count his errors of judgement on the fingers of one hand, it tasted like poison. He helped himself to another beer and angled her a challenging look as she mutely stared at him, her mouth half open in surprise.

'No,' Tess agreed stiffly. Now that she was looking at the detail, she could see that his hair was rumpled and he looked a bit *askew*—a bit like a guy who wasn't completely in control of everything around him. Vulnerable, it struck her. 'If you'd wanted to spend time with your girlfriend, then a group outing might not have been the best idea. Or did you think that I would be a good buffer between your girlfriend and your daughter?'

Matt tilted his head back to swallow some beer and continued to stare at her.

Held reluctant captive by those dark, brooding eyes, Tess felt her skin begin to tingle—and she hated the feeling. It reminded her of how weak she had been to allow this man to climb under her skin. She hated the intensity of his silence. It felt as if he was sifting through her thoughts, turning her inside out and exposing all her doubts and weaknesses. He already seemed too capable of forcing her to face up to failings she hadn't known existed.

'Well?' She angled away from him and sank into one of the kitchen chairs. 'I got the impression that Vicky hadn't had a lot of contact with Samantha.'

'Almost none,' Matt agreed.

'So what was the grand plan, Matt? To get the nanny to pave the way for a happy family unit? Take some of the heat off your girlfriend?'

'Vicky was never a contender for a happy family unit.' He had been leaning against the wall. Now he pushed himself away, dumping the empty beer bottle on the counter *en route* to a chair, which he sat on, his big body indolent and relaxed under the influence of drink. Not too much, but certainly enough to paper over the sharp edges of his mood.

'Well, that's none of my business,' Tess muttered. Of their own volition, her eyes flicked towards him, taking in all the details of his body, and she realised that there was a familiarity to what she was seeing that was scary.

'Turns out—' he laughed shortly, stretched out his legs and stuck his hand in his trouser pocket '—that I was on my own when it came to that misconception.'

'I don't know what you're talking about. Have you been drinking?'

'Now, what would give you that idea?' His eyes locked with hers and there was a lazy amusement there that made her go hot and cold. Even when she hurriedly looked away, she could feel him *looking* at her in a way that he hadn't looked at her before—looking at her in a slow, leisurely way that made her want to fidget. 'I let that relationship get out of hand,' Matt mused. 'I took my eye off the ball. While I was under the impression that we were having a casual fling, it turns out that Vicky was making all sorts of plans.'

'What sort of plans?' Tess was fascinated to hear more. Matt had never breathed a word about his personal life, but she wasn't looking at the Matt she knew. She was tiptoeing on the very edge of seeing a side to him that hadn't been in evidence before, and she was eaten up with curiosity.

'Are you having fun?' He laughed softly under his breath and Tess flushed.

'Of course not! *You* came here, don't forget! And if you want to talk, then that's fine by me.'

'I actually didn't come here to talk about Vicky,' he murmured. He shifted in the chair, leaned back into it. 'You distract me.' He enjoyed the way she blushed madly when he said that, and leaned forward as though not quite believing her ears. 'You make me lose track of what I want to say.'

'*I'm* not making you lose track of anything,' Tess said briskly, but there was slow burn inside her that felt good.

'Oh, right. It's the demon drink. I'll stick to the agenda, in that case. My daughter has reverted to her old ways.' He leaned forward abruptly, elbows on thighs, and pressed his thumbs against his eyes.

His body language spoke a thousand words and Tess automatically moved towards him, hovered for a while, not quite knowing what to do, and eventually pulled her chair so that she was sitting right alongside him. Should she reach out and try to comfort him? Confused and addled, she opted for sitting on her hands.

'What do you mean?'

'I mean…' Matt looked directly at her and raked his hand through his hair. 'We got back to the apartment and she promptly proceeded to shut herself in the bedroom.'

'But didn't you go in to try and talk to her?'

'Of course I went in! She lay there with her back to me and her headphones stuck in her ears—and, *hell*, I can't *force* her to have a conversation with me, can I?'

'So what did you do?'

'I had a couple of whiskies in rapid succession. It seemed like a good idea at the time.'

'And Vicky…?'

'Dispatched. The point is, I'm back to square one.' His smile was tight and bitter. 'It seems that the ground I believed I'd covered was just a bit of wishful thinking.'

'That's not true!'

'No? Then perhaps you'd like to explain my daughter's lack of response?'

'She's ten years old! She's not capable of thinking things through in an adult way. She's had a disappointing day. I suppose she thought that she would have you to herself…'

'You mean have *both of us*…'

'No,' Tess said firmly. '*You*. She didn't bank on your girlfriend showing up, and she really didn't bank on her—I don't know—being so proprietorial…'

'Nor did I,' Matt muttered under his breath. Vicky had made *plans*! A stint in the Far East together, his daughter conveniently dispatched to a boarding school somewhere… She had even checked out possible acquisitions he could make once they were living in Hong Kong! He had been furious and appalled, and then had turned his wrath against himself—because, as he had told Tess, he had taken his eye off the ball and had reaped his just rewards. But his relationship with his daughter was the biggest casualty of his slip-up, and damn if he knew how he was going to rescue the situation.

'Samantha's not…'

'Not *what*?' he gritted into the developing silence. 'No need to tread on eggshells, Tess. I've already blown it. I think it's fair to say I can withstand whatever you have to say.'

'You haven't blown it! It's just that Samantha… Well, I don't think she ever really understood why she saw so little of you over the years.'

'She's told you this?'

'In bits and pieces. I mean, please don't think that we sat down one day and had a heart-to-heart, because we didn't. I don't think children of that age ever do. I don't think they know *how to.* But I've gleaned it over time.'

'You've *gleaned* it? And how did you respond?'

'What could I say? You've never spoken to me about your marriage…and, anyway, it wouldn't be my place to have that conversation with your daughter. That's something you would have to do. I thought, I guess, that you would. In time.'

'God. What an unholy mess.'

He looked wiped out, and she reached out and tentatively put her hand on his shoulder. When he responded by taking hold of it, she assumed it would be to politely dismiss her gesture of sympathy, but instead he kept hold of it, playing idly with her fingers with frowning concentration.

'Catrina and I were the perfect couple on paper.' Matt glanced at her, but Tess wasn't sure that he was seeing *her.* 'Our families knew each other. We moved in the same circles and came from the same background. I suppose you could say that there was an understanding—and the understanding was hastened along when Catrina fell pregnant. I wasn't gutted. Yes, I was young, but I was content to marry, and marry we did. With all the pomp and ceremony that vast wealth can buy. The cracks opened up almost immediately. Catrina was a socialite. I was an ingrained workaholic. She saw no reason why I should put time and effort into making money. As far as she was concerned my job should have been to lead the life of a playboy. Go skiing in winter for a couple of months. Take long summer holidays at her parents' house in the Bahamas. Take up golf. Lead a life that would complement hers.'

Tess tried and failed to picture Matt taking up golf and having long holidays. He was still playing with her hand, and it was doing all sorts of strange things to her body. Whilst she was desperate to concentrate one hundred percent on what he was saying, part of her was wrapped up with the tingling in her breasts, the dampness spreading between her thighs, the warm feeling in her belly that made her want to sigh and close her eyes.

'The more she nagged, the faster I withdrew into the

safety of work. We were a divorce waiting to happen, but I'm not sure it would have if I hadn't found out that my best man at the wedding had stepped in to carry out the duties she felt I was failing to do.'

Tess couldn't imagine what that would have done to a man as proud as Matt.

'My divorce was what dictated the relationship I developed with my daughter, and so here we are.' He gave her a crooked smile. 'Any thoughts?'

CHAPTER FIVE

'I DON'T understand. Surely the court would have awarded you joint custody, Matt?'

'A vengeful wife has a lot of tools at her disposal when it comes to making free and easy with court judgements,' Matt told her drily. 'Weekends were cancelled on a whim. I lost count of the number of times I travelled to Connecticut only to find that Catrina had taken Samantha off on a trip, destination unknown, leaving a bewildered maid to try and explain in broken English that there would be no visit that weekend. Toys were routinely left at an empty house. I never knew whether Samantha got them or not.'

Matt's eyes glittered with open pain and bitter regret. This was a man who opened up to no one, and Tess wasn't sure whether this flood of confidence and self-recrimination was something he would live to rue, but she stroked his face with a trembling hand while her mind frantically spun off at another devastating angle.

While she had been busily telling herself that what she felt for Matt was an understandable case of lust, she had failed to recognise that it ran much deeper than that. She had long stopped being a concerned spectator to someone else's problems. She hadn't forsaken her social life because she lusted after Matt Strickland and was driven to spend as much time in his company as she could, like a lovelorn teenager. She had forsaken her life because she had unwittingly become sucked into his. It had been easy, at first, to dismiss him as the sort of man who took advantage of everything and everyone around him, but slowly but surely she had begun glimpsing other sides of his complex, absorbing personality.

She had watched him subdue his natural inclination to dominate so that he could make strides in getting to know his daughter. She had been ensnared by a wit and intelligence that was far greater than she had originally imagined. She had been seduced by those snatches of humanity she saw in his less guarded moments.

She had fallen in love with the whole man, and the time she had spent ignoring that reality hadn't served to protect her—it had just rendered her horribly defenceless.

Looking back now, Tess could see that love had just been waiting round the corner, ready to ambush her and turn her world on its head. Matt Strickland had overwhelmed her. She had been waiting for something gentle and careful, and had been unprepared for the chaos and power of real love, gutsy and demanding, when it finally came. She had expected that the guy who won her heart would be kind and sensitive. She had been utterly unprotected against a man who'd broken through to her heart like a battering ram and grabbed it when she hadn't even been looking—when she hadn't even taken the time to steel herself.

Her heart was racing. Inexperience left her unsure as to what to do. She had never considered herself extraordinary because she hadn't fallen into bed with any man. It just had never happened, and she had accepted that with a shrug of her shoulders.

'My relationship with Samantha became distant,' he said heavily. 'Stilted. Nothing I did, when I *did* manage to see her, could reverse the effects of the separation, and God only knows what Catrina had been telling her when I wasn't around. And just when I thought that some progress was being made…*this*…!'

'You came here,' Tess murmured.

'Where else? You know the situation better than anyone.'

He gazed at her with those stunning eyes and her breathing became laboured. Without warning, the atmosphere shifted. She could sense him grow still. It was impossible to think straight and nor could she tear her eyes away from his dark, outrageously sexy face. She wanted him so badly that it was a physical pain inside her, and her craving was made all the more irresistible because of the intensity of the emotion underlying it. She leaned forward and kissed him very chastely on his cheek, and the shock of contact almost had her reeling back.

'It'll be all right,' she whispered huskily. 'Samantha may have been disappointed at the way today turned out, but you've already started building the blocks of a relationship with her and she'll have that to fall back on.'

She was losing herself in the intensity of his gaze, and with a soft moan she did the unthinkable. She placed the palm of her hand on his chest and leaned into him once again. This time her kiss—not on his cheek, but daringly, recklessly, on his lips—was sweetly lingering, and an exquisite rush of pleasure crowded her mind, driving coherent thought away, taking away the ability to analyse what she was doing. She felt that if she stopped breathing just for a second she would be able to hear the frantic beating of her heart.

It didn't occur to her that she might be making a complete fool of herself. She had acted on impulse and she didn't regret it.

When he curved his hand at the nape of her neck and pulled her towards him she melted into the embrace as though this was the moment she had been born to savour.

This wasn't why he had come. Was it? He knew that she had been the first person he thought of in his frustration. He had called his housekeeper and had been waiting by the door for her to arrive so that he could come here and do…*what*?

What had he been expecting? At the back of his mind, had he already succumbed to the desire to take her to bed? From every angle, seeing Vicky had been a disaster. Not just from the point of view of his daughter. He had looked at her standing next to Tess and suddenly he hadn't been able to remember what he had ever seen in the woman.

Her statuesque beauty now seemed angular and unappealing. Where Tess was soft, her face open and transparent, Vicky was a hard-bitten career woman. He had been bored by her monotonous monologues about the Hong Kong market, impatient with her informed conversation.

Had he come here because he had been driven by something more than just an urge to offload?

The fact that he had even felt the need to offload was, in itself, cause for wonder.

The honeyed moistness of Tess's mouth was driving him crazy, but he still managed a final last-ditch attempt to control the situation.

'What's happening here?' He pushed her away and his resolution was immediately floored when he felt her tremble against him. 'We…shouldn't be doing this.' His voice was rough and uneven.

'Why not?'

'Hell, I can think of a hundred reasons!'

'You're not attracted to me…?'

'That's not one of them.' His mouth hit hers with a hunger that detonated an explosive pleasure inside her that she had never known existed. Her whole body was suddenly on fire and she could hardly sit still. She needed to wriggle just to try and assuage the burning restlessness blazing a trail through her.

'I'm not about to make love to you in a kitchen!' Matt growled, and Tess whimpered, her eyes fluttering closed, as he lifted her off the chair and began heading towards a bedroom—mistakenly kicking open the door to Claire's room first and then, two seconds later, getting it right.

He deposited her on the bed and she lay there in a state of heightened excitement, watching as he closed the curtains and then fumbled with his belt, finally whipping it off in one swift pull.

Released from the mindless intoxication of his body

being in contact with hers, she felt the reality of her virginity penetrate through to her fuddled brain.

This was a situation she had never envisaged, and there was no ready process she could think of for dealing with it. She just knew that she was beyond the point of walking away. And it felt *right*, she told herself fiercely. She was in love with him! She wasn't going to listen to any little voices in her head trying to push their way to the surface and preach to her about consequences. She wasn't—because there were always consequences to everything. If she didn't do this—if she turned her back on this one moment in time—then she would forever live with the consequence of that. Would forever wonder what it would have been like to surrender to this big, powerful man who had stolen her heart.

Optimistic by nature, she pleasurably played with the thought that this could lead anywhere. Who was to say?

He had stripped off his shirt. Her breath caught in her throat and she drank in the muscular beauty of his body. When he moved, she could see the rippling of sinew and the raw definition of his torso. He reached for his zip and she nearly fainted in anticipation. Her clothes were an irritating encumbrance, but she lacked the courage to divest herself of them.

He walked slowly towards her and she squirmed. Her eyes flickered away as he tugged down the zip and she heard the soft drop of his trousers, the sound of him stepping out of them, and then she was looking at him, shyly at first, and then mesmerised by the massive surge of his powerful erection.

With small, squirming movements, she edged up

into a sitting position and hooked her fingers under her vest.

'I've thought about this,' Matt muttered in a driven undertone, and her eyes widened in surprise.

'You have?'

'Why so shocked? You're sexy as hell. You must know the effect you have on a man… No, don't lift a finger. I want to take off your clothes piece by gradual piece.' He gave her a slow, curling smile that made her bones melt, and then he straddled her.

She fascinated him, and suddenly he could barely wait a second longer. Like a horny teenager, he covered her body with his own and kissed her with bruising ruthlessness, his hand moving along her thigh and easily slipping underneath the silky trousers. She was as soft and as smooth as satin. Just the feel of her was enough to wreak havoc with his control, and he had to slam the door shut on his raging libido or else risk making a fool of himself.

She wasn't wearing a bra. He had spotted that the second he had walked through the door. He caressed her full breasts through the thin, stretchy fabric of her vest, felt the way they moulded into his big hands and the way her nipples were tight and stiff under his fingers. He wanted to do this slowly, to take his time, and was disconcerted to realise that he had been fantasising about this for weeks. It had never risen to the surface of his consciousness but it must have been nagging at the back of his mind, and touching her now had released the nebulous, intangible notion. His hand shook as he heaved himself up so that he could pull off the vest with one hand.

'God, you're so damned beautiful,' he rasped, bending to nuzzle one breast, teasing her nipple with the tip of his tongue while she panted and moaned.

Having thought that he had barely noticed her as belonging to the female sex, Tess allowed herself to fully occupy Cloud Nine. He wanted her. He thought that she was beautiful. For the moment it was enough, and as she squirmed underneath him, desperate to get rid of her clothes, she felt herself letting go.

She pushed her fingers into his hair and urged his head down so that he could fiercely suckle her pouting nipple. He grappled with her trousers, levering himself up so that she could wriggle herself free of them.

His effect on her was electrifying. She felt as though this was what her body had been designed for—to be touched by this man. She arched upwards and cried out helplessly as he continued to move his mouth over her breasts. She ran her hands across his shoulders and felt the bunched muscles. She couldn't seem to remain still. When she angled her body up her nakedness touched his, and his stiff erection against her was explosive.

Tess had had boyfriends in the past, but none of them had ever affected her like this. Indeed, she'd had no desire to submit her body to theirs the way she wanted to submit her body to this man. She had enjoyed kissing, and there had been a bit of amateurish fondling, but this was in a league of its own, and her body sang under his expert touch.

He parted her legs with one hand, and as he continued to lavish attention on her breasts he began to move his hardness between her thighs, driving her into a frenzy.

'Talk to me,' he commanded hungrily, and Tess looked at him, confused.

'About what?'

'About how much you want me. I want you to tell me...' He laughed softly, and then demonstrated exactly what he meant by talking to *her*, telling her how much he wanted her and what he wanted to do to her. All the time his hard, pulsing erection pushed between her parted legs. Tess was going out of her mind.

'I want you...*now*...' she groaned, when she thought that she wouldn't be able to take any more.

'I'm not finished enjoying you yet.' He gradually began trailing an erotic path down the length of her body, relishing the salty taste of her perspiration on his tongue. Her uncontrolled passion matched his own and he liked it. As with everything she did, she was generous in her lovemaking. He realised that it was what he had expected. She didn't hold back. Her personality was forthright, open, giving. Her lovemaking was the same, and it unlocked a barrage of mindless desire he hadn't been aware he possessed.

He paused as he neared her thighs, and reared up to support himself on his hands so that he was looking down at her, appreciating her soft, feminine mound which was slick with moisture. The sweet, honeyed, musky smell of her threatened to tip him over the edge—and that was before he even touched her. Which he fully intended to do. With his hands, with his fingers, with his mouth, until she was begging for release.

He blew softly against her and Tess gasped. She was discovering a whole new side to herself, and she wouldn't have been able to stop herself now even if she had wanted to. She didn't think that she had ever known what it was like to have a man turn her on—but then she had never *met* a man like Matt.

She froze as he gently parted the delicate folds of her femininity, and sank back with a soft sigh of pleasure as he darted his tongue between and tasted her. She covered her face with one arm and her mouth fell open. The sensation was so exquisite that she could hardly breathe. All the muscles in her body seemed to go limp and she gave herself over to his gentle, persistent mouth which continued savouring her.

His dark head between her legs was the most erotic thing she had ever seen in her whole life. His exploring mouth became more demanding, and she could no longer keep still. Her body was spiralling out of control.

But before she could climax right there, Matt heaved himself up.

'I need,' he muttered shakily, 'to get some contraception.'

'Please,' Tess whimpered, digging her fingers into his shoulder, because he just couldn't leave her *now* to start fumbling for a condom. Her periods had always been as regular as clockwork. She was as safe as houses and she needed him inside her *right now.* Her body was screaming out for it.

'I'm safe,' she gasped.

Matt needed no further encouragement. He really wasn't sure whether he had any contraception on him anyway. He was ultra-careful, always made sure to carry his own protection, but his sex-life with Vicky had been sporadic, and she had, anyway, been on the pill. He was uneasily aware that even if he hadn't had any, if she hadn't given him the green light, he might just have chanced it—because his body was on fire and the only way he could douse it was by taking her. He had never been so out of control in his entire life. For someone who had imposed stringent discipline in all areas of his life, because there was no such thing as a happy surprise, it was weirdly exhilarating to be suddenly and temporarily freed from the shackles.

He thrust into her with an intensity that made her wince and cry out in pain. Confused, Matt eased himself back. He was big. He knew that. And she felt tight—so tight that he might almost think…

'Are you a *virgin*?' he asked with dumbstruck incredulity, and Tess turned her head away.

After the initial discomfort the pain was receding fast, being replaced by a driving, burning need to feel him push into her again.

'Just carry on, Matt…please…I need you…'

'Look at me,' he growled. 'I'll be gentle…' His eyes held hers as he moved slowly and surely, building into a rhythm that took her breath away. However much he had teased her and touched her, in unimaginable places, to have him inside her was the greatest intimacy of all. Tess wrapped her arms around his waist and her body bucked as he moved faster and deeper. She felt his physical release just as her own body spiralled out of control, causing her to cry out and dig her fingernails into his back. His spasms as he ejaculated into her were the most wonderful things she had ever experienced.

She loved this man, and she had to resist the urge to tell him. She held that warm knowledge to herself, and there was a smile of pleasure and fulfilment on her lips when she finally shuddered one last time and then lay, spent.

Matt rolled off her and propped himself on his side to look at her.

'So…tell me about that…'

'Tell you about what?' Tess murmured sleepily. 'That was amazing. Was it…' She looked at him, suddenly anxious. 'Was it okay for you?'

'It was…pretty amazing. I was your first.'

'I'm sorry.'

'Don't apologise.' He smiled and stroked the side of her face. A *virgin.* A twenty-three-year-old virgin. He hadn't known they existed. 'I liked it. Why me?'

Tess drew her breath in sharply. 'I guess,' she said, reaching to hook her hand around his neck and nuzzle the dewy moisture there with her lips, 'you just really turn me on. I don't understand it, because you're not the type of guy I ever imagined myself going for, but when I'm near you I just seem to fall apart.'

'You might have guessed that it's the same with me,' Matt confessed a little unsteadily. He could feel his body confirming that admission, hardening again in record time. 'I should have been able to restrain myself, but…'

Tess felt him stir against her naked thigh and a heady sense of power filled her. But nudging its way through to her fuddled brain were snatches of uneasy recollection of how, exactly, they had ended up in bed together. He had come to talk about Samantha. Had he been drinking? He certainly hadn't been as composed as he usually was. It had been the first time she had seen him with all his barriers down, and his unexpected vulnerability combined with her fledging acknowledgement of how she felt about him had been an intoxicating mix. From being the girl who had stayed on the sidelines as her friends had all fallen into bed with guys they'd later avoided, or succumbed to languishing by telephones waiting for calls, she had gone to being a girl who had flung herself at a man because she just hadn't been able *not* to.

'Why should you have been able to restrain yourself?' she asked anxiously. 'Did I take advantage of you?'

Matt shot her a gleaming look of surprise. 'When you say things like that I feel about a hundred years old.' He laughed softly. 'Don't worry. I'm wonderfully adept when it comes to women cruelly trying to take advantage of me. I find it pays to just relax and go along for the ride.'

'You're teasing me.'

'I'm enjoying your lack of cynicism. When I came here, I was at the end of my tether. You relax me, and I like that.'

Tess wasn't sure if that was strictly accurate. It could be said that simply lovemaking had relaxed him. But she wasn't going to analyse the finer points of his remark. She was going to take it at face value because she had never felt so wonderfully, gloriously *complete* in her whole life.

She guided his hand to her breast, and he grinned wickedly and pushed her back against the bed, slung his thigh over hers. She felt the weight of it with a feeling of bliss.

'You're a fast learner.' His voice was thick with satisfaction.

This time their lovemaking was fast and hard. Matt liked giving pleasure. He knew just where to touch her and how to make her body respond. Shorn of inhibitions, Tess was his willing student. She wanted to be guided. She wanted to give him as much pleasure as he gave her. She was guiltily, horribly aware that she wanted a great deal more than he probably suspected, but for the moment she was greedy enough to take what was on offer.

Their bodies were slick when they were sated. In a minute Matt would have to leave. He would talk to Samantha in the morning. He told her this as she lay against him, her body naturally curving against his as though it had been fashioned just for that purpose. His admission that it would be an uphill task made her smile.

'Talking's not that difficult,' she breathed with drowsy contentment. 'Communication is the key thing when it comes to all relationships. I know that sounds like a cliché, but I think it happens to be true. Maybe...' she tested the water '...that's why your relationship with Vicky didn't work out...'

Matt shrugged. 'It doesn't matter why my relationship with Vicky didn't work out.'

Tess thought that it mattered to *her*. He had married the perfect person and it hadn't worked out. He had gone out with the perfect replacement and that hadn't worked out. Amongst her tangled thoughts she figured that if only she could pinpoint *why* the perfect exes hadn't worked out, then maybe—just maybe—she could avoid the mistakes her predecessors had unwittingly made.

She refused to accept that the most wonderful physical and emotional connection she had ever made with another human being was destined to be short-lived.

'She seemed very nice…' Tess persisted. 'And you must have had a lot in common.'

'Look.' Matt propped himself up and turned on his side to face her. 'Drop it, Tess. It's of no importance. Like I told you, I took my eye off the ball with Vicky. She started getting ideas.'

His face was shuttered. He was locking her out of this conversation.

'I guess it's understandable.' Tess tried to laugh. She was no good when it came to playing underhand games. She would have been hopeless at persuading a confession out of anyone, and it showed in the shaky tremor of her voice when she spoke.

Matt looked at her narrowly. Her upturned face was sweetly, delectably soft and vulnerable, and a prickle of unease curled in him. But the touch of her was so heady, and the feel of her was like a shot of adrenaline to his jaded palate…

In short, she was irresistible. But just in case…

'Vicky wanted a happy ending,' he said bluntly. 'It wasn't going to happen. I've been married once and I lived to rue the day. The only good thing to emerge from that disaster was my daughter. I'm not a candidate for a repeat performance. I'm telling you this because I don't want *you* to get any ideas.'

'You mean crazy ideas like Vicky got?' It was like being sliced in two. The path was forked and she was being given a choice. Follow the road he indicated or else walk the other way. If she had thought that a fleeting glimpse of his vulnerability indicated hint of softness, then she had been mistaken. The dark, fathomless eyes locked onto hers were deadly serious, and Tess very quickly made her decision.

Take what he was offering. She had fallen in love with him and she couldn't walk away. When had she ever been able to do anything by halves? She had given herself to him completely, and if it made no sense then that was something she would have to learn to deal with.

'I guess…well…she's in her thirties. Maybe she could hear her biological clock ticking away. But not me! At twenty-three, life is still a grand adventure, and I don't want you to think that I'm going to start demanding anything of you—because I'm not.'

It would be a disaster if he found out what she felt about him. One night of passion and a woman confessing undying love would be his nightmare. He would run a mile and he wouldn't look back. She would cease being the girl who could make him relax and would turn into a needy, clinging harridan who wanted more out of him than he was willing to give. Having never had much of a head for numbers, Tess could do the maths pretty quickly when it came to *this* particular scenario.

'In fact, like I said, you're not the type of man I would ever fall for,' she confided.

'I'm not…?'

'No! I may not be experienced, but I'm not foolish enough to think that lust has anything to do with love.'

'You just gave your virginity to me because…?'

'Because I wanted to. No one's really ever turned me on like…'

'Like me?' Matt interjected smoothly. 'I believe you. Lust can be powerful. Overwhelming. And maybe you came to New York looking for an adventure. Why else would you be using contraception? You're young, you're beautiful… Did you get bored where you lived?'

Tess was still lagging behind, wondering whether she should own up to the fact that she wasn't actually using any contraception at all but was perfectly safe anyway. Matt's low, seductive murmur seemed to be coming from a long way away. His clever mind was leapfrogging through what she had said and making its own deductions. She had come to Manhattan seeking adventure. She had been bored and restless. She had taken the necessary precautions not because she was desperate to lose her virginity but because she wanted to be prepared in case the situation arose. Perhaps she had been dazzled at the thought of Manhattan and everything and every*one* it could offer. That would make perfect sense to him. He was a man with a healthy sexual appetite. He would fully understand how, at the age of twenty-three, her virginity might have become an albatross around her neck rather than a treasure to be hugged until the perfect man came along. Hell, there was no such thing as a perfect soul mate anyway!

Tess half listened and made vague appropriate noises. For a man with a brilliant mind he seemed very good at arriving at all the wrong conclusions, but she knew that he had to. He had to make sense of her and slot her into a category that didn't threaten the pattern of his orderly life because he wanted her. He wasn't at all surprised that she had chosen to lose her virginity with *him*. He was supremely confident of his own sexual magnetism. His misguided conclusions and freewheeling assumptions even made sense in a weird, convoluted way.

She wasn't sure she recognised herself as this woman who knew what she wanted, was in search of sexual adventure, and had the good sense to go on the pill, throwing caution to the winds so that she could have a no-strings-attached relationship with him.

It would have been so much easier if she *had* been that person, she thought ruefully. Instead, here she was—not too sure what she was doing or what she had got herself mixed up in.

'So on Monday…' He kissed her with such leisurely, thorough expertise that she forgot how precarious her life had suddenly become. 'I'll make sure that I'm back by six. We'll take Samantha out for a meal somewhere. I'm hoping conversation might be back on the agenda with her. And afterwards…'

Tess felt the thrill of excitement. It flooded her veins like a toxin. It closed her mind to any question that she might be doing the wrong thing.

CHAPTER SIX

TESS stared in the mirror at the woman she had become in the space of four glorious weeks. The changes were slight, but *she* had no difficulty in noticing them. Matt Strickland had turned her into a woman. In a series of barely recognisable stages she had grown up. She dressed differently now. The trainers had been replaced with flats. The vests were a little less clinging.

'I don't want other men looking at you,' he had told her, with a possessiveness that had thrilled her to the bone. 'Is that a crime? When you wear those tight vests men look, and when they look I want to kill them. And don't even *think* of going anywhere without a bra. That is a sight to be afforded only to me.'

The vests had been replaced with looser silk tops that made her look sophisticated and glamorous, and she liked her new image. He claimed not to have an ounce of jealousy in his body, but when she had idly watched a man walk past a week ago, her mind a thousand miles away, he had tilted her face to his and told her, with a forced laugh, that he wanted her to only have eyes for *him*.

Tess stored and treasured all those passing moments. They had to mean *something*! He made no effort to conceal the fact that he wanted her. Sometimes, with Samantha between them as they ate dinner, she would glance up and find his eyes on her, and she would see naked hunger there. Her breasts might ache just at the sight of him, and she might feel that telltale dampness between her thighs, but she knew that her effect on him was just as powerful. He had told her that business meetings had become a minefield because just the thought of her could give him an instant erection.

Tess loved hearing things like that, because they seemed to indicate that something would come of their relationship—although she was smart enough never to let any mention of that leave her lips.

She had also made sure not to breathe a word to Claire. Nor had she mentioned it to her parents or any of her friends, whose lives seemed so distant now anyway.

At first she had worried that keeping it secret might be difficult. Claire had always been able to read her like a book, and she would have been able to chivvy it out of her without any trouble at all if she had smelled a rat, but in all events it had been much easier than expected. Tom had proposed, and Claire was residing in a parallel universe. She spent most of her time at his place, and disappeared on weekends to his parents' house in Boston, where a wedding planner was feverishly working to produce a magical wedding in six months' time. Even her parents skirted over what was happening in her life because they, too, were wrapped up in their contribution to the Big Day.

Menus were discussed and seating plans were debated and bridal magazines were pored over until Tess wanted to scream—because where was *she* going with her clandestine relationship with Matt?

Time was moving on. Her ticket to return to Ireland was booked for the beginning of September. But she could easily alter that. Her parents had lived for years in America before they'd moved back to Ireland. All three children had been born in America. Tess had dual nationality and she could have produced that, like a rabbit from a hat, at any given moment in time—but that moment had not arrived. Matt didn't talk about the future and nor did she.

But she would *have* to talk about it. She had spent weeks ducking below the radar and enjoying each day as it came. She could hardly believe that once she had been a girl who *had* lived her life like that, content never to dip her toes in the water.

Hence she was dressing with particular care tonight. Samantha was with her grandparents in the Hamptons for the weekend, and she and Matt would have the apartment all to themselves. It would be the perfect opportunity to discuss this *thing* they had, which had no name. She would use all the feminine wiles at her disposal. Wasn't all fair in love and war?

Her dress was a wonderful long affair in shimmering pale yellow. It fell softly to the ground and left her brown shoulders bare. Her shoes were delicate sandals with yellow straps.

The drive over gave her twenty-five minutes to plan what she was going to say and when. Just thinking about it made her nervous. She wondered whether he was still as allergic to commitment as he had once said he was, then told herself that that wasn't the most important thing, because she could stay on in Manhattan with him, looking after Samantha. She wouldn't actually be demanding anything. The words *a stay of execution* uncomfortably sprang to mind, but as quickly as they had taken shape they were dismissed, because she couldn't afford to let herself start being pessimistic.

Scrape the surface, though, and she was a bag of nerves by the time they reached his block of apartments and the elevator was silently transporting her to the top floor.

Matt had had a key to his penthouse cut for her, and occasionally she used it, but it had never felt right. She had been given a key to facilitate her job as Samantha's nanny. She wanted a key because Matt saw her as the other half of a couple and trusted her enough to come and go as she pleased. So now, as always, she rang the doorbell and waited in restless tension, clutching her little handbag in front of her.

When he pulled open the door her heart flipped over, as it always did, and for a few seconds she was completely lost for words.

He never failed to render her speechless. She saw him almost every day, had made love to him countless times, had watched, fascinated, the lithe suppleness and latent power of his naked body, and yet every time she laid eyes on him it was as if she were seeing him for the first time. He took her breath away, and however much he assured her that she had the same devastating effect on him she didn't believe him. Compared to the women he could have at the click of his fingers, she was just an averagely pretty face.

But she wasn't going to think like that. Not tonight, when she wanted to think positive.

The long look he gave her thrilled her from the crown of her head to the tips of her toes and she smiled shyly.

'Do you like it?' She stepped into his luxurious apartment and gave a little twirl. The dress followed her, as soft and tantalising as a whisper.

He caught his fingers in her hair and pulled her towards him.

'You look like a goddess,' he murmured. 'Some kind of exquisite, ethereal creature.' His finger was now tracing her bare shoulder and her body reacted with mindless excitement. She could already feel her nipples tightening, and her breasts were heavy and sensitive, in expectation of being touched by him. She felt faint thinking about his mouth circling her nipples and licking them until she could scarcely breathe.

But she pushed him gently away and walked towards the kitchen, from which was wafting a delicious smell.

'Have you surprised me by cooking?' she teased, putting some necessary distance between them because she didn't want the evening to start with them in bed.

'You know I don't do that.' She looked so damned edible standing there, delicate and fragile and breathtakingly pretty—an exotic counterpoint to the hard masculinity of his kitchen. He would have pinned her against the wall and taken her without preamble, but she had dressed to impress and he would savour the anticipation of getting her out of her clothes. 'My dependable caterers have done justice to some fillet steak and…' he came close, close enough for her to breathe him in, and lifted the lid of a saucepan '…some kind of sauce.' He remained where he was, dipped his finger into the sauce and held it to her mouth. 'Taste it and enlighten me,' he murmured, already so hot for her that it was beginning to get painful.

He lounged against the counter, his feet loosely crossed at the ankles, and gave her a look of burning satisfaction as the pink tip of her tongue licked the sauce from his upheld finger. Like a cat finishing the last remains of the cream.

'Brandy and peppercorn, I think. And I don't see why you *can't* cook for me now and again.' She gave a mock sigh of wistfulness. 'You're a perfectly good cook. I know. You've done lots of wonderful things with Samantha. Remember that risotto?'

'Correction,' Matt told her wryly, 'Samantha has done lots of wonderful things with me. My role is solely to do as I'm told.'

'Since when do you *ever* do as you're told?' She relaxed enough to smile, but tension was still blazing inside her.

'You can always put that to the test.' He leant against the counter, hemming her in. 'Command me, my beautiful little witch,' he breathed into her ear, before nibbling the side of her neck and sending a flurry of piercing, pleasurable sensations rippling through her. 'Would you like me to get down on my knees and push that sexy dress up so that I can drive you wild with my mouth? Hmm? Or we can always go for something a little more kinky…. It would appear that dessert comes with custard…'

'Stop it!' Tess laughed, hot and flustered, and feebly pushed him away—but he had set up a very evocative image in her head that she was finding difficult to dispel. 'We're not going to do any such thing.'

'Sure? Because I saw a flash of temptation in your eyes just then… Now, let me just see how much you dislike the idea…' To hell with not moving too fast and giving the dress time to have its moment of glory. Still supporting himself with one hand flat against the edge of the granite counter, he reached down and inched the silky fabric upwards. His eyes didn't leave her face.

'You have no self-control, Matt Strickland,' Tess protested weakly.

'Tell me about it. And what about you? I'd say we're even on that score.' He felt the softness of her thighs. The cloth was bunched around his hand and he shrugged it away as he dipped his fingers beneath the lacy band of her thong and slipped them into her.

Tess melted. Her eyelids fluttered shut. This wasn't playing fair! She blindly searched for his mouth with hers, but after just a fleeting kiss he pulled back and whispered, in a sexy, velvety voice, 'No chance. I want to see your face when you come…'

'Okay. You win,' she groaned jerkily. 'But let's go to the bedroom…make love…ah…' She couldn't finish the sentence. Her body was moving of its own accord. Her head was flung back and her eyes were shut as his fingers continued to plunder her, moving fast and hard, then slowly and gently, teasing every ounce of sensation out of a body that felt as limp as a rag doll.

Colour climbed into her cheeks and her breathing became laboured, and then she was falling over the edge, shuddering with the power of her orgasm and crying out, at which point Matt brought his mouth against her so that he could breathe in the wildness of her groaning.

'That,' he murmured when she had climbed down from the mindless heights of pleasure, 'is an excellent way to start any evening.'

Under normal circumstances Tess would have been in enthusiastic agreement with that statement. Matt knew just how to excite her in unimaginable ways. But tonight she had another purpose, and as soon as she had smoothed down her dress she was back to feeling as nervous as a kitten.

Without looking for ways to be critical, she realised that he was utterly oblivious to her mood—but then thoughts of her leaving would probably not have crossed his mind. For weeks Tess had nurtured the hope that what they had would leave him wanting more. They shared a lot together. He might be ruthless and driven in the work place, but with her he had been tender and thoughtful, and with Samantha he had shown boundless patience and a resilient ability to take the knocks and somehow find a way of turning them around. Would he be able to give her up without a backward glance? She had subconsciously chosen to think that he wouldn't, but now, as he whistled softly and made a great show of doing things with the pots and pans, she wasn't sure.

If he was that tuned in to her feelings then surely he would have picked up on the fact that she was more subdued than usual?

Now he was chatting to her about work. He sometimes did that, even though he had once commented wryly that he really didn't know why he bothered, because the second he started he could see her eyes glazing over.

She accepted the drink that was proffered and settled on one of the leather dining chairs at the kitchen table. He was fairly useless in the kitchen. A tea towel was slung over one shoulder and every cooking utensil seemed to be out, even though he was really just heating up a variety of dishes. In between stirring things and peering under lids he chatted and sipped his wine, occasionally glancing round at her, and even in the midst of her anxious thoughts she still warmed at the hot possessiveness in his eyes.

'But do you miss it?' Tess asked abruptly, as a plate of food was placed in front of her with exaggerated flourish. 'The long hours, I mean? For weeks you've managed to be pretty sensible about getting back here in time, to see something of Samantha, so do you miss the work you would have been putting in otherwise at the office?'

In the middle of topping up their glasses, Matt paused and looked at her. Something uneasy stirred in him, but he quickly put that to rest by telling himself that nothing was amiss. She might be a little quieter than she normally was, but she had melted at his touch the way she always did. He never seemed to tire of her helpless excitement whenever he touched her. It turned him on in ways that he no longer bothered to question.

'That's a strange question. I work for several hours after Samantha has gone to sleep. It's satisfactory.'

'So…does that mean that you've restructured your life?'

'Where are we going with this conversation?' Matt

tried to keep the irritation out of his voice. He had become accustomed to her undemanding nature. It suited him. She was always happy to fall in with whatever he wanted, and over the weeks he had discovered that her lack of complication suited him in ways nothing else seemed to have suited him in the past, but there was something insistent about her at the moment that seriously threatened to ruin the atmosphere.

'It doesn't have to go anywhere,' Tess told him, picking at her fillet steak. Her appetite was fading fast. 'I'm just asking.'

Matt pushed back his chair and tossed his napkin on a plate of food that was only half eaten. 'I haven't restructured my life.' He linked his fingers behind his head and looked steadily at her flushed face. 'I'm in the process of trying to find a balance.'

'Does that mean you thought it was out of sync before?'

'It means that Samantha is a reality I have to deal with. Originally I thought that I would more or less be able to carry on as normal, with a great deal of help to cover for my absences. It wasn't a viable option. It's a necessary sacrifice and it's been worth it. Whether I'll be able to carry on being consistent remains to be seen. There will be instances when I have to go abroad, and I'll have to get overnight cover when that arises. My mother would be happy enough to come here for a few days, so I don't foresee any problems that won't be surmountable. Now, does that satisfy your curiosity?'

'I wish you wouldn't act as though I'm being a nuisance just by trying to have a conversation with you!' Tess heard herself snap, shocking herself by daring to rock a boat which she had steadfastly tried to keep level for the past two months. But she could no longer help the build-up of anxiety inside her. Once upon a time she had never had a problem in saying what she thought. This was like walking on eggshells. One false move and she sensed that the structure she had built around herself, the little fortress in which she had placed Matt and Samantha, would be shown for the house of cards that it really was.

She was finding it hard to hold on to her sunny optimism.

'What's going on, Tess?'

'Sometimes I like to think that there's a little more to us than just sex…'

The silence stretched endlessly between them, straining until it was so close to breaking point that she could hardly breathe. She certainly couldn't look at him. Instead she fiddled with the fork on her plate, making swirly patterns into the fast cooling brandy sauce which she had hardly tasted.

She looked up when he began clearing the table, and had to resist the temptation to fling herself at him and tell him that she was just kidding. She knew that she had embarked on this relationship with the understanding that she would demand nothing, and she had been good to her word, but she had fallen deeper and deeper and deeper in love with him. She realised now that she had vaguely assumed that time would sort them both out and provide a way forward for their relationship.

When she stood up to help him, her legs felt wobbly. She was relieved when he told her to wait for him in the living room.

She was so absorbed in her thoughts that she wasn't aware of him framed in the doorway until he spoke. She twisted round to look at him.

'You were saying…?' Matt prompted, strolling into the living room to join her on the sofa.

Tess was finding it difficult to reconcile the man looking at her now with a closed, shuttered expression with the man earlier, who had laughed into her mouth and caressed her with such gentleness that she had felt as though they were two halves of the same person.

'I was saying that I'd like to think that what we have is more than just sex.' She smoothed her hands nervously along her dress. 'Do you care about me at all? I guess that's what I'm asking.'

'What kind of a question is that? If I didn't care about you I wouldn't be having a relationship with you.'

'So I'm on a par with Vicky? Is that what you're saying? You care about me the way you cared about her?'

'I prefer not to make comparisons between the women that I sleep with.'

'What's the difference between us?' Tess persisted doggedly.

Matt glared at her. He didn't like being hemmed in, and as someone who had never made a habit of giving an account for his actions he was infuriated that she was persisting with this line of questioning.

'For a start, Vicky never had a relationship with my daughter.'

'But if you take Samantha out of the equation…'

'How *can* I take her out of the equation? She's part of my life.'

'You know what I'm saying,' Tess insisted stubbornly. Having come this far, she was committed to this course of action whatever the outcome.

'No. I don't.' Matt couldn't believe that the evening to which he had been looking forward with impatience and anticipation was collapsing into a mess of awkward questions and unreasonable demands. They should have eaten a very good dinner, drunk some excellent wine, chatted with the ease with which they always chatted, and then progressed into bed where he would have lost himself in her. The fact that she had seen fit to scupper his plans ratcheted up his foul temper by a couple of notches.

'Okay, then I guess I'd better spell it out for you. I know you don't like the thought of planning ahead. *I know that.* The only stuff you ever seem to think about long-term is stuff to do with your work. You can think fifty years in advance when it comes to arranging your work life!'

'There's nothing wrong with that,' Matt gritted, avoiding the unwelcome topic of conversation that was staring him in the face. 'Businesses don't function on a let's-see-what-happens-next basis! Foundations have to be laid and plans have to be followed through.'

'I understand that. But I just want to know where your personal life features in all that foundation-laying and following through. Where do *we* feature in all that? I need to know, Matt, because I'm due to leave America in a couple of weeks…'

Pinned to the spot, Matt refused to be told which direction he should take. He had embarked on a fling with her and had spared little thought for the temporary nature of what they had. She was due to leave the country and, since he wasn't into long term situations, the nebulous matter of her departure didn't impinge at all on his conscience.

He had been clear as to what he wanted and she had readily agreed.

Hell, hadn't she come to America to sort herself out? Hadn't she gone on the pill because she had been willing for an adventure?

He uneasily cast his mind back to her shyness—that tentative, easygoing, sunny disposition that he still found endearing. His notions of her being a wild girl let loose in a big city had been crazily misplaced. Suddenly, like a jigsaw puzzle coming together with the final piece, Matt faced the truth that he had effectively spent the past few weeks subconsciously dodging, and he blanched at it. He had wanted her, and he had therefore talked himself into getting what he wanted by closing his eyes to the obvious.

'What do you want me to say?'

'I…I can stay on if you want me to. I've been giving it a bit of thought. It's not as though I have a job to go back for, and I love working here—working with Samantha. I know when she starts school she won't need me to be around during the day, but that doesn't matter. I could look around for something to do here. You see, I have dual nationality, so that wouldn't be a problem…' Her voice trailed off and she sifted her fingers through her hair and looked at him. 'It's not as though I would *live* here or anything…' The sound of her pride being washed down the drain was as loud as a fog horn in her ears. 'Claire would be happy to have me continue to stay with her. She's hardly ever around, anyway…she spends so much time with Tom. In fact, I would probably be doing her a favour…looking after her place when she's not there…'

'This isn't what we signed up for, Tess.'

The gentleness of his voice brought a lump to the back of her throat. He was letting her down and making sure not to be brutal about it. But at the end of the day being let down remained the same, whether it was done brutally or not. She sat on her hands, not trusting herself to speak for a few fraught seconds.

'I know. I never wanted to get involved with you…'

'Because I'm not the type of guy you ever saw yourself getting involved with.'

'Right. But…' She lifted her eyes bravely to his face and swallowed hard. 'I did. I let myself get involved with you and I just need to know if there's any chance for us.' She couldn't bring herself to tell him that she had fallen in love with him. He didn't want to hear anything she was saying. It was written all over his face. 'Even though,' she qualified gamely, 'it isn't what either of us signed up for.'

Matt was still. A series of flashbacks was playing in his head like a very rapid slideshow. His wife, his marriage, his resolve never to put himself in such a position again. The women he had dated since then had been ships in the night, and he had enjoyed having it that way. He had determined not to take on commitments he knew he would eventually dislike and resent. However ideal the woman in question might seem, it would only be a matter of time before she was shorn of her halo and revealed to have all the needs and expectations that would be guaranteed to drag him under.

And was Tess the ideal woman anyway?

She had never held down a job aside from this one. She had spent her life cheerfully drifting, content to live in the shadow of her sisters. She wasn't independent. She was hopeless when it came to most things of a practical nature. Her personality was so diametrically the opposite of his that he sometimes had to take a step back and marvel.

Yes, those differences were charming at the moment, but they would irritate him on a long-term basis. He was sure of it. Nor, he admitted to himself, did he care for the fact that she was, in effect, offering him an ultimatum. Ask her to stay or else watch her walk away. Matt didn't like ultimatums. He especially didn't like them insofar as they applied to his private life.

'You have some time remaining here,' he heard himself say brusquely. 'Why start asking about the future? Why not just enjoy what we have?' In his way, it was as close as he could come to expressing his feelings. He could promise her nothing.

'What would be the point?' Tess cried out with anguished feeling.

'So in other words,' Matt filled in, his voice unyielding, 'unless I can promise you marriage, you see no reason to stick around?'

'I told you…I don't *want* marriage…'

'Come off it, Tess! Are you going to tell me that you would be happy to get a part-time job over here and shack up in your sister's apartment just so that you could be at my beck and call?'

'I wouldn't see it that way,' she muttered inaudibly.

'I'm honest enough to tell you that you would be making a big mistake.' Feeling suddenly restricted, Matt stood up and paced through the room. She had effected small changes in the time she had been coming to the apartment. There was a little frame of some pressed flowers she had done with Samantha. Some of her CDs had found their way over and were sitting on his antique sideboard. A handful of pictures had been developed, and she had framed those and arranged them on the windowsill. He glared at all those intimate touches, which he had never asked for but to which, he thought bad-temperedly, he had become accustomed.

'We've had fun together. I would like us to continue having fun together until you leave. But if you don't want to then that's your choice.'

He hardened himself to the sound of her silence. He wasn't ending this because he was cruel. He was ending this because he was a hell of a lot more experienced than she was and he could foretell the mistake it would be even if she was wilfully choosing to close her eyes to it.

He needed to lead by example, and he would. It was what he had always done. It didn't feel good, but he couldn't allow himself to give her false hope. *More* false hope. Because it was obvious that she had been mulling over their situation longer than she had let on.

Mind made up, he turned to look at her. He brushed aside a momentary feeling of panic and clenched his jaw.

'You're going to have to be strong to take what I'm going to say now, Tess. We're not suited for one another.

You're right when you say that your choice of ideal man would be the opposite of someone like me. I have a hell of a lot more experience than you, and trust me when I say that I would drive you round the bend.'

'What you're saying is that *I* would drive *you* round the bend.' She breathed in deeply, angry with herself for having revealed so much, and angry with him for his patronising tone of voice. 'You don't mind sleeping with me, but I'm just not good enough for you to have a proper relationship with!'

Dark colour accented his high cheekbones. 'This has nothing to do with whether you're *good enough* for me or not!' he roared, losing control.

She was searching around for her bag, which she located in the kitchen. 'I still have a couple of weeks left working for you.' She held her head up high. 'I'd really appreciate it if I could see as little of you as possible.'

'That,' Matt said tightly, 'can be arranged. Consider yourself relieved of your duties.' Angry frustration ripped through him. He could barely look at her, and yet at the same time was driven to watch in glowering, hostile outrage as she headed towards the door, only pausing when her fingers were curled around the doorknob.

'Would you mind if I at least said goodbye to Samantha?' she asked jerkily, and Matt nodded an affirmation.

Which meant that there was nothing left to be said. It had all gone horribly, catastrophically wrong, but indecision pinned her to the spot until she told herself that it was pointless.

She closed the door quietly and firmly behind her.

CHAPTER SEVEN

DESPERATE to convince Claire that she was on the mend, Tess lay in bed trying to think happy thoughts.

For the first time in two months, she was rudderless. She literally felt like one of the walking wounded. She had told Claire that she felt she might be coming down with something. Actually, she *did* feel she might be coming down with something. She had woken up every morning—every morning for five interminable days, during which time she had heard nothing from him, not a text, not a phone call—with a vague feeling of nausea.

She no longer knew how to plan her days, and no longer had any interest in doing anything, anyway. She would be leaving the country in just over a week, and all she really wanted to do was hibernate. She wanted to scuttle somewhere dark and safe and warm, like a mole, and sleep until the memory of Matt had faded from her consciousness, allowing her to pick herself up and carry on.

She finally understood how much she had allowed him to become the axis of her entire universe. In a matter of just a couple of months she had given away all of her carefree independence, and now that the umbilical cord had been slashed she was floundering like someone deprived of oxygen. She missed him. She missed Samantha, with whom she spoke daily. She had seen her two days previously, and had obviously looked so dreadful that her mumbling something about *being a bit under the weather* had been one hundred percent convincing.

Claire had been sympathetic to start with, and had made a production of keeping her distance.

'I can't afford to catch anything,' she had apologised. 'Life's too hectic at the moment for me to take time out with an infection.'

Tess was beginning to think that she might actually be *willing* herself into a state of ill health. She could barely keep a thing down. If things continued in this manner she would have to be ferried back to Ireland in an air ambulance.

However, now, after five days, Claire was running out of patience.

Tess still lay with her eyes closed, telling herself that her nausea was all in her mind, when the bedroom door was flung open.

'It's nearly ten-thirty!' Claire was dressed to go shopping in one of her signature summer outfits—a silky short dress which would have cost the earth and a pair of complicated gladiator-style sandals—and was munching on a sandwich the size of a brick.

Tess tried to duck under the duvet.

'You can't *still* be under the weather, Tess!'

'You know I've never been a morning person.' She averted her eyes from the sandwich because it was making her stomach lurch.

'Well, it's Saturday, and you're coming shopping with me. You can't spend the rest of your time here feeling sorry for yourself because you have a bit of a stomach bug! You'll get back to Ireland and you'll kick yourself because you wasted your last week and a half. Might I remind you that there's *nothing to do* back home?'

'I'm going to do that teaching course. I told you!' After years of never settling down to anything, one good thing, at least, had come of her stay in Manhattan. She had been pushed into coming to New York so that she could find direction, and she had.

'Well, whatever,' Claire dismissed bracingly, 'you're still going to get out of that bed and come shopping with me—because tonight you're coming to a party! And I've already got a ticket for you so don't even *think* of telling me that you can't go because your tummy hurts! We're going to get you something glamorous and wonderful and you're going to *have a brilliant time*!'

That was Claire-speak for *do-as-you're-told-or-you-won't-hear-the-end-of-it.*

'I'll give you half an hour, Tess, and then I'll expect to see you up and ready to take on Manhattan!'

Tess had no idea where they would be going that night. She obediently spent the day traipsing behind Claire, making a heroic effort to show enthusiasm over the clothes that were paraded in front of her and being compelled to try on. At five-thirty they returned to the apartment and she was instructed to 'get your act together and change as quickly as possible because the taxi's booked for seven.' She was also instructed to *look happy*, because there was nothing worse than a party-pooper.

Tess did as she was told because she knew that her sister had a point. She really would have to start moving on. She couldn't continue to feel sorry for herself indefinitely. Matt had never promised her anything. He had never, ever given any indication that what they had would extend beyond her stay in America. *She* had been the one guilty of misinterpreting their relationship. She had flung herself headlong into something that defied all common sense and had started building castles in the air because she had been naïve.

When she thought logically about it, she and Matt stood on opposite sides of a great divide. He was the sophisticated, accomplished and confident product of a birthright of wealth and power. Not only had he grown up within the cocoon of a privileged background, but he had expanded a thousandfold on his fabulous inheritance. He had taken over his father's massive business concerns and diversified and branched out because it was in his nature. He was too clever to stand still and so he hadn't.

Compared to him, she was the equivalent of a minnow swimming next to a Great White. In her calmer moments she grudgingly conceded that there had never been a chance for them—not in any real sense of the word. Even if he had loved her madly—which he hadn't—it would still have been a big deal for him to have committed to someone so far removed from his own social background.

So moving on was her only option.

When she was fully dressed she could almost feel confident that she was beginning to. At least she *looked* the part—which was some of the battle won, if nothing else.

Claire rapped on the bedroom door at six-thirty and after twenty minutes of clinical inspection pronounced herself satisfied.

She had ended up buying an off-the-shoulder long dress, deep green in colour, which was gathered at the bust and then fell to the ground. It should have made her look shapeless, but it didn't.

'You have the boobs for it,' Claire had said approvingly, when Tess had emerged from the changing room. 'And the colour goes with you complexion.'

It was a style that couldn't be worn with a bra, and Tess found herself thinking back to Matt's possessive reaction to any thought of her going braless in public. She had found it so intoxicating at the time, and had read too much into it.

Now, she felt a welcome spurt of rebellion as she followed Claire out to the taxi.

It was a forty minute drive to a building which, she was told, was actually a very well known art gallery that rented out its premises for a select few. Outside a crowd of people, dressed to kill, were entering in an orderly line, showing tickets to two doormen.

Inside, the party was in full swing. The art gallery was über-modern. A large, brilliantly white reception area branched out on either side to two massive rooms. In one, a quartet played melodious jazz music. In the other, people networked. There was the feel of a very expensive warehouse about the place. The walls in both the rooms adjoining the reception area were painted a pale slate-grey and adorned with large modernistic works of art. The lighting comprised thousands of spotlights which, to Tess' relief, were dimmed to a mellow glow. It was like nothing she had ever seen before, and for a while she actually forgot her misery.

Tom was waiting for them, and he and Claire both made a big effort to introduce her to people, but after fifteen minutes Tess could see that her sister was becoming bored with playing babysitter. She shooed her away because, actually, she was quite happy to wander around looking at the art work, and after a while she slunk into the room with the jazz band, so that she could sit and listen to the music.

She had tucked herself at a table at the back of the room, with a glass of champagne in front of her, and was listening to a very perceptive song about unrequited love when a low, familiar voice behind her made her freeze in the act of raising the glass to her lips.

She spun round and half stood. Just one look, one second, told her that she had not even begun to put Matt behind her. He was formally dressed and was wearing a red bow tie—the only splash of colour against the blackness of his suit and the crisp whiteness of his shirt.

'What are you doing here?' Tess asked, in a daze.

'I could ask *you* the same question.' He had seen her from behind, walking into the room with the jazz musicians. There must be at least three hundred people at the do. Not only were the rooms on the ground floor crowded, but upstairs several more rooms were filled with employees and important clients. It had been pure coincidence that he had seen her, because he had spent most of his time upstairs, preferring the arrangement of comfortable leather sofas and chairs to the cocktail party atmosphere of the rooms on the ground floor. However, there had been no mistaking that caramel hair falling down her slender back as she weaved a path through the crowds. For a second he had been shocked enough to lose track of what was being said to him by one of the directors at his Boston office. Then he had made his excuses and followed her.

It irked him that he had not been able to get her out of his head. Everything he had said to her had made perfect sense, and yet she was still managing to infiltrate his waking moments with irritating consistency—like a high-frequency noise that had managed to lodge itself in his head, disrupting his thought patterns and making him lose concentration at inconvenient times.

Of course it had only been a few days, and her absence had been made doubly worse by the fact that Samantha was constantly talking about her. She had accepted the fact that Tess had left. She had known that her stay in America would come to a close, and it was a source of unending relief to Matt that his daughter was in a much better place than she had been a few months ago and so had found it easier to adapt to the young student who had replaced Tess for a few weeks. But she still mentioned Tess daily. Matt had been forced to make noises about plans for Tess returning for a visit, perhaps the following Easter. Maybe sooner! He had been obliged to grit his teeth as he was shown all the photographs they had taken together. He had listened, nodding in agreement, as he was told how much Grandma and Grandpa would have loved her.

He hadn't been allowed to forget the woman! Little wonder that he had found himself following her into this room, standing for a while to watch as she leant forward at a table, one hand idly curled around the stem of a champagne flute, the other cupping her chin as she tapped her feet to the quartet.

If he had been stupid enough to worry about her, he now scowled as any questions on that front were answered. She looked on top of the world. In fact she looked a knockout. And it was clear that she had come to pick up a guy. Why else would she be wearing something that left her shoulders bare and moulded the fullness of her breasts with such loving perfection?

Tess was completely and utterly thrown by the sudden appearance of Matt. It was as if her feverish mind had summoned him up.

'I…I came with Claire,' she stammered, before remembering that she was in the process of *moving on* and therefore letting herself go weak at the knees at the sight of him just wasn't going to do. But he looked so *sexy.* Had he come with someone? Even if he hadn't, he would surely be *leaving* with someone. All eyes were on him, sidelong glances, but then he *was* head and shoulders above every other man at the party.

He was also in a bad mood, and her spirits deflated because she knew why. He had come to a party and the last person he wanted to bump into would be *her*, when he thought that he was well and truly rid of her.

'I never expected to see *you*!' Tess forced herself to laugh. 'What a coincidence! But I guess Manhattan is smaller than you think! Mary says that London is like that! She'll be out having a drink somewhere, and before she knows it she recognises someone!'

'Pull the other one, Tess. You must have known that

I was going to be here.' Matt swallowed the contents of his whisky in one, and dumped the empty glass on the table at which she was sitting. He shoved his hands in his pockets. Did she think that he was going to stand here and make nice with a lot of polite conversation? Well, he wasn't in the mood.

'Why would I know that?'

'Because this is a company do. *My* company do, not to put too fine a point on it. So telling me that you had no idea that I might possibly attend my own party doesn't really wash.'

'*Your* party…' Claire hadn't mentioned it. She didn't know the circumstances of her departure from Matt's employment. Tess had told her that she had contracted a bug, and that with only a short period of time left had been given leave to get well and then enjoy some time out by herself rather than spend her remaining days working once she recovered. Claire would have expected her to have known about the party, and as Tess had asked no questions Claire had offered no information beyond the fact that it was a very dressy affair.

Matt's lips curled as he looked down at her generous breasts, pushing against the soft dark green fabric. 'Is that why you made a point of coming?' he rasped. 'You knew that I was going to be here and you thought that it would be a good opportunity to show me what I was missing? Well, it won't work.' All of a sudden he needed another drink. He glanced around, frowning, and like magic a waiter bearing drinks on a large circular tray appeared. Matt took a glass of wine, though he would rather have had a whisky, and drank half.

Tess had got lost trying to work out what he was attempting to say to her.

'I *didn't* know you were going to be here,' she protested truthfully. 'Claire never mentioned that it was a company do!' She was adding up the implications behind his remark, which had been delivered in a derisive tone of voice targeted to offend, and she was suddenly shaking with anger. 'And even if I *had* known that you were going to be here—*which I didn't*—I would *never* have come here to…to show you what you were missing!'

'No? Then why the over-the-top sexy dress? Not to mention the fact that you're not wearing a bra!'

The mere mention of that did horrible things to her body, reminding her of how easy it was to respond to him even when he wasn't touching her. Even, it would seem, when he was being rude and arrogant and insulting.

'This isn't for *your* benefit!' Her nipples were throbbing and she was mortified at her reaction. She felt that he must be able to see what he was doing to her with those laser-sharp, all-seeing black eyes of his.

'No? Because, like I said, it won't work. I've seen that ploy too many times. It's lost its effect over the years. We're no longer involved, and the best thing you could do for yourself is to move on.'

'I can't believe how arrogant you are, Matt Strickland! I…I can't believe what I ever saw in you!'

'I would bet that it wouldn't take much to remind you.'

The look in his eyes had changed suddenly. Tess's breath caught sharply in her throat. That simmering, *hot* gaze was not what she needed—not now! Did it give him a kick to put her meagre will-power to the test? To prove how much of a hold he still had over her? She wanted to weep in frustration.

Perversely, Matt was relishing this hostile clash of words. He had been chatting and socialising like a man on a tour of duty—looking covertly at his watch, mentally bemoaning the fact that the party still had hours to run. Now he was having fun, in a grim, highly charged sort of way. And he couldn't peel his eyes away from her delectable body. If there hadn't been a roomful of people watching, he would have been sorely tempted to remind her of just what she had seen in him! He pictured himself yanking down that flimsy piece of nothing shielding her glorious breasts, cupping their fullness in his big hands, teasing her nipples with the abrasive pads of his fingers.

From where the memory had been lying, close to the surface, he recalled their last evening together, when he had brought her to a shuddering orgasm in the kitchen of his apartment. He had a graphic flashback to the feel of her body writhing against his fingers. He could even recall the soft fall of that yellow dress she had been wearing.

'Has it occurred to you that I *am* moving on?' Tess lied, tossing her head and trying hard to remember the name of the guy who had badgered her for a while and slipped her his business card.

No. Quite frankly, it hadn't. Nor was he having a good time assimilating the concept.

'Maybe,' she threw at him defiantly, 'you're really not the reason I wore this dress—considering I didn't know that you were going to be here anyway! In fact, for your information, I've already been asked out on a date!'

That was a red rag to a bull. Having just told her that she should move on with her life, Matt underwent a rapid turnaround and was outraged that she should be out on the prowl within *seconds* of their split.

'Who by?' he demanded, keeping his voice well modulated, although inside he was seething with what could only be termed *jealousy.* His weakness infuriated him.

'Tony!' The name came back to her in the nick of time. 'Tony Grayson.'

Sales manager. His career now looked perilously short-lived. Matt drained his glass, flicked back the sleeve of his shirt to look at his watch. 'Well,' he drawled with lazy indifference, 'good luck with that one. I should be careful if I were you, though. New York isn't a small village in Ireland. Give off too many obvious signals and you'll have to be prepared to take the consequences. In other words, don't go near the fire unless you're happy to get burnt.'

He turned on his heel and walked away. Like a punctured balloon, Tess felt herself deflate. She could no longer put on a show of having fun. She just wanted to leave, to get back to the apartment. Like a patient suffering a severe relapse, she needed immediate time and space to recover, because seeing Matt again had knocked her for six.

Knowing that Claire would feel obliged to try and persuade her to stay, she didn't bother to look for her. Instead, she took the coward's way out and texted her a message. By the time she checked her mobile phone Tess would be at the apartment, in her pyjamas.

Three days later, Tess emerged from the doctor's surgery on wobbly legs. At Claire's insistence, she had finally gone.

'You can't climb on a plane feeling under the weather!' Claire had announced, in that voice of hers that permitted no argument. 'The flight back is a nightmare—it's so long, and if you start feeling really poorly on the plane it's going to be awful. You obviously have some kind of persistent stomach bug and you *have* to go to my doctor and get it sorted. If you like, I can come with you.'

Now Tess was weak with relief that she had turned down her sister's offer to accompany her. What would she have said if she had been confronted with the news that Tess was pregnant?

In a daze, she went to the nearest coffee shop and sat down, unseeing, in front of a cappuccino which, having ordered, she no longer wanted.

Her initial reaction—one of sickening disbelief—had ebbed. Now it was replaced by a recognition that all the signs had been there. She had just missed them. After their first time together, when she had been so convinced that there had been no danger of her falling pregnant because she was as regular as clockwork, she had gone to Claire's doctor—the very same doctor who had broken the news to her twenty minutes ago—to have a contraceptive device inserted. The pill would have been easier, but Tess had an aversion to tablets.

'You must be very fertile,' the doctor had said, while Tess had sat here like a statue, trying to absorb what had just been said to her. She had been thinking that it certainly explained her dodgy stomach. A quick look in her diary had confirmed that her period had been late—something she hadn't even noticed because between being on Cloud Nine and then catapulted back down to Planet Earth she just hadn't been thinking straight. In fact, she hadn't been thinking at all.

Across from her, a woman leaned over and asked if she was all right and Tess returned a wan smile.

'I've just had a bit of a shock,' she said politely. 'I'll be fine once I drink this cup of coffee.'

Of course she would have to tell Matt. He deserved to know. But just thinking about that brought her out in a cold sweat of nervous perspiration.

Their last bruising encounter had left her in no doubt that he was over her. He had given her her walking papers and instructed her to move on—because he had. He had spoken to her in the patronising tone of someone dealing with a nuisance who showed promise of becoming a stalker. He had accused her of dressing to attract him, and she knew, deep down, that he hadn't believed a word she had said about not knowing that he would be at the party. He wanted nothing further to do with her and what was he about to get? A lifelong connection that he hadn't engineered. He had trusted her because she had told him that she had taken care of contraception, and in return for his trust he would find himself a father in a few months' time.

But to keep the truth from him would be immoral.

Without giving herself the opportunity to dwell on what she knew she had to do, Tess stood up and hailed the first cab to his offices. If she thought too much about it she would think herself into a change of mind. She was having his baby.

The traffic, as usual, was gridlocked, and Tess was a bag of nerves by the time she paid the cab driver and looked up at the offices that commanded one of New York's prime locations in the heart of the financial sector.

She had been to his office several times before—little visits with Samantha—so she was recognised at the vast reception desk and waved across to the bank of elevators, one of which would take her to the top floor of the thirty-four-storeyed building.

His offices were the working equivalent of his apartment. Luxurious, plush, silent, industrious. His own office, perched at the end of the thickly carpeted corridor, was as big as some people's flats, with one section partitioned for his personal assistant and another, larger one, comprising a comfortable sitting area with leather chairs and plants and little tables. She knew that there was even a bathroom adjoining his office, for those times when he came in very early or was obliged to leave very late.

It struck her forcibly that the size and the opulence of it was a glaring reminder of just one of the many differences between them.

Thinking like that made her feel even more nervous, and she tried to project a composed demeanour as she stopped to chat to his secretary.

He wouldn't be aware that she was even there, and Tess was tempted to give him just a little bit longer to enjoy his carefree life before she blew it to smithereens.

Matt, buzzed eventually by his secretary, felt a kick

of satisfaction knowing that Tess was waiting to see him. She had been on his mind even more, having seen her at that party. He didn't know what she wanted, but when he thought that she might actually be reconsidering her options he felt like a predator in full and final control of its elusive prey. Maybe she had gone to the party to meet a man, but he had thought about that and eventually dismissed the notion. It really didn't tally with what he had come to know about her. At any rate, he liked to think that seeing him had made her realise what she really missed. She would only be around for a few more days, but he was more than willing to reluctantly set aside his pride and take her back to his bed. In fact—and he barely acknowledged this—it was a shame that she had made the fatal mistake of trying to tie him down, because who knew what might have been the next natural step for them…? He might just have offered her the very thing she had so obviously craved…

He didn't immediately look up when she quietly entered, although his senses went on sudden red alert. When she cleared her throat he finally raised his eyes, and then sat back in his chair without saying a word.

'I'm sorry if I'm disturbing you…' she began, painfully aware of his lack of welcome. He might just as well have set a timer on his desk and told her that she had one minute to state her case.

'You're lucky to find me here,' Matt told her politely. 'I have a meeting in a matter of minutes, so whatever you've come to say, you need to say it quickly.'

Faced with such bluntness, Tess dithered in an agony of uncertainty. She had vaguely rehearsed what she might say, but now she was looking at him every single thought vanished from her head. She felt possessed of roughly the same amount of confidence as a rabbit staring at two headlights bearing down on it at great speed.

'Well?' Matt said impatiently. 'What is it? I haven't got all day.'

'Even if you had, I still don't think I'd find this easy to say,' Tess told him shakily.

Something in the tone of her voice infused him with ominous foreboding. He went completely still and waited.

'You're going to be mad, but…I'm pregnant…'

CHAPTER EIGHT

MATT froze. He wondered if he had misheard her, but then immediately revised that notion as he looked at her face. She was white as a sheet and leaning forward in the chair, body as rigid as a piece of wood. *Mad?* She thought that he might be *mad*? That seemed to be the understatement of the century.

'You can't be,' he asserted bluntly, and Tess flinched.

'You mean you don't want me to be—but I am. I did a test this morning. In fact, I did more than one test.'

His usually sharp brain seemed to have shut down. Nothing had prepared him for this.

'You were protected,' he told her flatly.

With an abrupt movement that took her by surprise, he propelled himself out of his chair and walked towards the window. For once, his natural grace had deserted him.

'If this is some kind of ruse to get money out of me, then you can forget it!' He leant against the window and then restlessly began to prowl the office. He couldn't keep still. Running through his head was the thought that this just couldn't be happening.

'Why would I be using a ruse to get money out of you?'

'You can't accept that we're finished. You want to walk away with more than just a few memories. You *know* how much I'm worth!'

'I don't know how you can say that!' Tess exclaimed, dismayed. 'Since when do you know me to *ever* think about money? And I wouldn't make something like this up!'

No, she wouldn't. Painful sincerity was etched on her face. Whether he liked it or not, she wasn't lying. She was carrying his baby, and that was a fact with which he would have to deal whether he liked it or not. While he tried to scramble for some other explanation, he was already accepting the truth that had been forced upon him.

But beyond that there were still a lot of questions to be answered, a lot of perfectly reasonable suspicions to be dispelled—if, indeed, they could be. Surfacing through the fog of his confused thoughts, a line of pure logic crystallised, and in the face of that every natural instinct he possessed took second place.

She had bewitched him, made him behave in all sorts of ways that had been alien to him. Yes, he had had a good time with her. She had known how to make him laugh and she had relaxed him in a way no other woman had. But in the bigger picture how much did that really count for?

He had known her for a couple of months! And lo and behold, having assured him that she was fully protected, here she was—pregnant and knowing full well that her future would now be a gold-plated one. Did that make sense? Wasn't there something strangely suspicious about the circumstances?

Matt slammed the door shut on any shady areas in this scenario. He was conditioned to be suspicious. It was his protection. He wasn't about to abandon it now, even if he could see the glisten of tears in her eyes. He reached for the box of tissues he kept in his drawer and handed them to her, but there was a cold cast to his features that sent a chill to her heart.

'So. Explain.'

'That first time…'

Matt cast his mind back with a frown. 'If I recall, you assured me that—'

'Yes, I know what I said!' Tess interrupted fiercely. 'Okay. I lied.' Her eyes skittered helplessly from his dark, incredulous face.

She was aware of him picking up his phone, talking in low tones to his secretary, knew that he was telling her that he didn't wish to be disturbed. While he spoke, she did her best to get her tangled thoughts in order.

'That didn't come out right,' she said, as soon as he was off the line. Nervously, she plucked a tissue from the box on her lap and began shredding it with shaking fingers. 'It wasn't so much a lie as…I economised a bit with the truth. When you asked me whether I was taking any contraception, I was so…so turned on that I didn't want us to stop…'

Without warning Matt's mind did an abrupt detour and swerved off back to that night when they had made love for the first time. He had never been so turned on in his life before. Even thinking about it now… But, no, there was no way that he was going to let his body dictate his handling of this situation. He didn't care how turned on she had been. She had deliberately lied—taken a chance with life-altering consequences attached.

'So you decided to let me go ahead. You *risked a pregnancy* for a moment of passion. You threw away your virginity and played fast and loose with both our lives because you *just couldn't help yourself...*'

'I didn't *throw away* my virginity. I gave it away. I gave it to you because I wanted to—because you were the first man to make me feel like that. I've always had a very regular cycle. I honestly thought that there would be no consequences.'

'I'm flattered that you were so overwhelmed by me that you just couldn't help yourself, but excuse me for thinking of a more prosaic reason that you hopped into bed with me.'

Tess looked at him in confusion. Everything about him was designed to threaten, and she didn't know whether he was aware of that. She had to twist in the chair to follow his movements, and her neck was beginning to ache from having to look up as he towered over her—a cold, distant stranger who had sliced through the fragile bridge that had once connected them. Her heart was breaking in two.

'Yes, I concede that you were turned on. But maybe it occurred to you that if you had to lose your virginity with anyone, why not lose it to someone who was a damn good financial bet? If I recall, I gave you every opportunity to take a step back, but maybe you didn't want to lose the chance. Maybe, subconsciously, you didn't mind playing with fate, because if you did get pregnant then it would be a very profitable venture for you...'

Anger brought a rush of colour to her cheeks. 'A

profitable venture? You think I *wanted* to get pregnant? You think I *want* to have a child at the age of twenty-three, when I'm just finally beginning to see a way ahead for myself? I was actually thinking about going into teaching! I was going to work with children because I got so much pleasure from working with Sam. I was going to go back to school and try and get the qualifications I should have got years ago! Do you really think that I *want* to ditch all of that?'

She stood up, trembling. She shouldn't have come. She had messed up his wonderful life. She should have just returned to Ireland. He would never have known about the pregnancy. In fact, she should never have got involved with him in the first place. She should have taken one look at the fabulous trappings surrounding him and realised that he was not in her league and never would be.

'I'm going to leave now,' she mumbled, frantically trying to hold on to her composure. 'I just thought that you needed to know…and now you do.'

She began walking towards the door. She didn't get very far. In fact two steps. Then Matt was standing in front of her—six feet two inches of menacing male.

'*Going to leave?* Tell me that was a joke.'

'What else is there to say?'

Matt stared at her as though she had taken leave of her senses—maybe started speaking in tongues.

'You've dropped a bomb on me and you *don't think that there's anything more to say?* Am I dealing with someone from the same planet?'

'There's no need to be cruel and sarcastic. It's…I'm dealing with the same shock as you…'

Matt raked his fingers through his hair and shook his head, as though trying to will himself into greater self control.

He was shaken to his very foundations. Had he felt the same way when Catrina had declared herself pregnant with Samantha? He had been so much younger then, and willing to drift into doing the right thing. Since those youthful days a lot of lessons had been learnt. He had erected barriers around himself and they had served him well.

Now he was staring at a problem, and whether he liked it or not it was a problem that would have to be dealt with. But all problems had solutions, and flinging accusations at the woman who was going to be the mother of his child would get neither of them anywhere.

And how clever had he been to accuse her of ulterior motives? Now she was staring at him with big, tear-filled green eyes, as if he had morphed into a monster, when in fact he had just reacted in the way every single man in his position would have reacted under similar circumstances.

That didn't alleviate the niggle of guilt, but he firmly squashed that momentary weakness.

'I don't feel comfortable having this conversation here,' he told her shortly.

'What difference does it make where we have the conversation?' Tess looked down at her feet, stubbornly digging her heels in. She didn't want to go to his apartment. Nor did she want to go to Claire's apartment. For starters, Claire knew nothing of what was going on. Right now she was on a job in Brooklyn, but what if she and Matt went to the apartment to continue their conversation and Claire unexpectedly showed up?

Tess knew that sooner or later everything would have to come out in the wash, but right now she felt equipped to deal with only one horrendous situation at a time. Her mind just wouldn't stretch further ahead.

In truth, she wanted to be somewhere as public and as impersonal as possible. It seemed to make things easier to handle.

'This is my place of work,' Matt intoned, already taking it as a foregone conclusion that she would follow his lead by heading towards the jacket which was slung over the back of one of the leather chairs. 'I've instructed my secretary not to disturb me, but a lot of meetings will be cancelled. Sooner or later she will come in and expect some kind of explanation from me, and when she doesn't get a satisfactory one she'll be curious. Frankly, I would rather not generate public curiosity in my private life.'

'What will you tell her?' Tess reluctantly conceded his point. He was an intensely private man. 'I'm not going to Claire's apartment and I won't go to yours.'

'Why not?' Matt paused and looked at her through narrowed eyes.

Heat shimmered through her. Alone with him… She didn't want her strength to be put to the test. She knew how weak she could be when she was around him. She had to build up an immunity, and enclosed spaces would be the worst possible start to doing that. If he could be considered an illness, and falling in love with him some kind of terrible virus that had flooded her entire system, then detachment was the first step to a possible cure.

'Are you suddenly scared of me?' he asked softly. 'What do you think I'm going to do?'

Tess shamefully thought that the danger would be *wanting* him to do things that he shouldn't do and she definitely shouldn't want. Given a lifebelt, she clutched it with both hands. Hadn't he accused her of the most horrible things? That being the case, why shouldn't she accuse *him* of a few?

'I don't know!' she flung back in a shaky voice. 'You've insulted me. You've as good as told me that I set everything up—that I took risks because I wanted to trap you. You've been a bully. Of course I don't want to be anywhere with you, unless there are lots of people around.'

'Are you saying that you're afraid that I might be physically threatening?'

'No, of course I'm not…'

A dark flush had accentuated his high cheekbones. 'I have never laid a finger on a woman before, whatever the provocation. The thought of it alone is anathema to me!'

'I'm tired,' Tess muttered wearily. 'I don't want to be badgered. Maybe you should just think about things overnight and then we can speak tomorrow. Or the day after, even.'

Matt didn't bother to dignify such delaying tactics with a response. He had never been a believer in putting off for tomorrow what could be done today. Problems not faced head-on, he had discovered to his personal cost, never went away—they just got out of hand.

'Wait for me by the lift,' he instructed her, 'I will need to discuss rearranging my schedule.'

'Really, Matt. There's no need to put your entire day on hold! Just let me go home and we can both discuss this when it's sunk in and…and we're both calmer.'

'I'm perfectly calm. In fact, given the situation, I couldn't be calmer.' Nor was he lying. The fog was beginning to clear and a solution was presenting itself. It was the inevitable solution, but already he was coming to terms with it. He was rising to the occasion and that, for him, was something of which to be proud. She would discover soon enough that he was a man who shouldered his responsibility—even when, as in this instance, it was occasioned by something out of his control.

Strangely, he didn't feel as cornered as he might have expected.

Tess regarded him helplessly. He could be as immovable as a block of granite. This was one such occasion. 'Then we'll go to a café. Or a coffee shop. Or even just find a bench somewhere.' When he nodded, she gave a little sigh of resignation and left him slipping on his jacket, shutting down his computer, getting ready to face one of the most important conversations of his life.

It was pointless pushing the button. He was with her in less than five minutes. He had told her that he was calm and he looked calm. Cool, calm and composed. If nothing else, he was brilliant when it came to hiding his feelings. In fact, he could have been nominated for an award, judging from the performance he was putting on as he depressed the button and they took the lift down.

There was a coffee shop two blocks away, he was

telling her. It would be relatively quiet at this time of day.

When she asked him, stiff and staring straight ahead like a mannequin, what he had told his secretary, he shrugged and said that he had intimated some sort of situation with his new nanny. Nothing new there, he had implied to her. It had been a thirty-second conversation. His secretary wasn't paid to ask intrusive questions.

As the lift door purred open, Tess thought that anyone listening to their impersonal, polite conversation would have been forgiven for thinking that there was absolutely nothing amiss.

Matt continued to talk to her as they walked towards the coffee shop.

He certainly didn't think he had overreacted to a word she had said, but he had still managed to scare her—and that didn't sit right with him. To think that she had looked at him with those wide green eyes and effectively informed him that she didn't want to be in his company without the safety of an anonymous public around her had shocked him to the core.

It was essential to put her at ease. Talking about nothing in particular as they covered the short distance to the coffee shop was step one in that procedure.

Once there, he installed her at a table away from the window and any possible distractions and ordered them both something to drink and eat—although when he appeared with two lattes and a selection of pastries Tess glanced at him and blushed.

'To be honest, I've gone off coffee,' she confessed. 'And food in general. I have morning sickness that lasts all day, pretty much.'

Which made it all so real that his eyes were drawn to her still flat stomach. His baby! Unlike the Matt of ten years ago, this Matt was finding it strangely pleasurable to contemplate impending fatherhood—even with the dilemmas involved. There was much to be said for maturity.

'I can get you something else. Name it. Whatever you want.'

'You're suddenly being nice. Why?'

Matt sat down and helped himself to a cinnamon roll. 'If you think that I reacted too strongly, then I apologise, but this has come as a shock. I've been very careful when it comes to making sure that…accidents never happen…'

Tess hung her head in guilty shame. And, as luck would have it, this 'accident' had occurred with a woman who had never been destined to be a permanent fixture in his life. He might not have lasted the course with Vicky, but Tess couldn't imagine that he would ever have accused *her* of staging a pregnancy for his money.

'However,' Matt continued, interrupting her train of thought before it had time to take hold and plunge her into further depths of misery, 'there's no point dwelling on that. We're both facing a problem and there are always solutions to problems. Have you told anyone about…this situation?'

'I've only just found out myself!' Claire didn't have a clue as to what was going on. She would be in for a double shock. Tess shuddered just thinking about it. When she paused to consider her parents, her mind went blank. Beyond that, there were so many practical concerns that she hardly knew where to begin—and here he was, cool as a cucumber, working it out as though it was a maths question with an easy answer.

'Well, sooner rather than later, that's going to have to change. Your parents are going to have to know, for a start.'

'Yes, I *realise* that...'

'How do you think they're going to react?'

'I...I haven't thought about it. Yet.'

'And then there's the question of money.' He watched her carefully, but she was obviously still mulling over the thought of breaking the news to her parents. He knew that she was very close to them. He could see where her thoughts were going. 'Fortunately for you, I am prepared to take full responsibility for this. I think you know where this is leading.'

Cinnamon roll finished, Matt looked at her over the rim of his mug and said nothing until he had her full and undivided attention.

'We will be married. There is no other option.'

He waited for signs of relief and gratitude. Now that his proposal had been made, he decided that things might have been considerably worse. Their relationship might have come to an end, but that end had been prematurely engendered by the fact that she had given him an ultimatum—by the fact that time had not been on their side. Yes, he had certainly concluded that she was not his ideal match, at least on paper, but his thinking had had to change and change it had. Never let it be said that he wasn't blessed with an ability to get the best out of a thorny situation.

Relief and gratitude were taking their time, and Matt frowned at her. 'Well? We're going to have to proceed quickly. I will break it to my parents, and then arrangements can be made for a wedding. Something small would be appropriate, I think you'll agree.'

'Are you *proposing* to me?'

'Can you think of a better solution?' Matt was prey to a one-off, very peculiar feeling. He was a knight in shining armour, she the damsel in distress. He had never been given to fanciful notions of this nature, but he was now, and a sensation of general wellbeing spread through him with a warm glow.

Her eyes glistened and he whipped out his handkerchief—pristine white.

'This is everything I ever dreamed of,' Tess said bitterly. 'And I'm not going to embarrass you by bursting into tears in the middle of a coffee shop, so you can have your handkerchief back.'

'I guess it is,' Matt concurred.

'All my life,' Tess continued in a driven undertone that finally caught his attention, 'I've dreamt of a man proposing to me because he has no choice. What girl wouldn't want that? To know that a guy who doesn't love her, and in fact was glad to see the back of her, is big enough to marry her because she's pregnant!'

For a few seconds Matt was stunned into speechlessness. Twice in one day so far he had been lost for words! Tess wondered whether a world record had been set.

'Furthermore,' she carried on, 'haven't you learnt *any* lessons from your past?'

'You're losing me. Correction. You've *lost* me.' Having leant forward, he now flung himself back in the chair and gave her a scorching look from under his lashes. 'I can't think of a single woman who wouldn't be jumping up and down with joy at this juncture! Not only am I *not* walking away, I'm positively offering a solution. You are having my baby. You will therefore be protected—as will our child. With my ring on your finger you will never need or want for anything in your life again. And what *lessons*,' he added belatedly, 'are you talking about?'

'I'm talking about your ex-wife, Matt! Catrina?'

'What about her?'

'You married her because she fell pregnant. You married her out of a misguided sense of responsibility.'

'I married her because I was young and foolish. Her pregnancy had very little to do with it.'

'Look…' She took a few deep, calming breaths. 'I understand that you want to do the right thing but the right thing, isn't for us to get married.'

'You're telling me that a stable home life for a child is unimportant?'

'You *know* that's not what I'm saying,' Tess cried in frustration. 'Of *course* a stable home life is very important for a child! But two people living under the same roof for the wrong reasons doesn't make for a stable home life. It makes for…for bitterness and resentment. It wouldn't be right for both of us to sacrifice our lives and a shot at real happiness because I happen to have fallen pregnant.'

Matt was finding it hard to credit that she was turning him down, but turning him down she was. Only days ago she had been desperate to prolong their relationship, and now, when he was offering her the chance to do so, she was throwing it back in his face as though he had insulted her in the worst possible way! On some very basic level, it defied understanding.

'You're not being logical.'

'I'm being incredibly logical. I won't marry you, Matt. I know I wanted us to carry on seeing one another—I know I would have stayed here a while longer if you had wanted me to—but I've had time to think about that, and you were right. It would never have worked out. We just aren't suited, and we're not going to become magically suited just because I made a mistake and fell pregnant.'

Matt felt the ground shifting awkwardly under his feet.

'You won't be returning to Ireland.' He delivered this with brutal certainty. 'If you think that you're going to make your bid for happiness across the Atlantic, then you're going to have to think again.'

A shot at real happiness? He pictured her having her shot at real happiness with one of those sappy guys she claimed to be attracted to and it was a picture that made him see red. He wasn't going to get embroiled in a long debate about it, however. Reluctantly he admitted that he was in a very vulnerable place. The second he had arrived at his solution to their problem, the very minute he had understood what would have to be done and had reconciled himself to the inevitable with a great deal of largesse, he had expected her to follow suit.

'Then I guess we'll have to talk about arrangements,' she said heavily.

Matt shook his head in the impatient gesture of a man trying to rid himself of something irritating but persistent.

'I would never deprive you of having a bond with

your child,' she continued gently. 'I know what you went through with Samantha.'

'So what are your suggestions?' When it came to the art of compromise, his skills were remarkably underdeveloped, but now Matt understood that compromise was precisely what he would have to do. Until he could persuade her round to his point of view. Legitimising their relationship made perfect sense to him, but he knew that he would have a lot of ground to cover. He had sidelined her, and she wasn't going to let him forget that—even though circumstances had now irrevocably changed.

Like a dog with a bone, he chewed over her assumptions that they were better off apart, that they were ill suited to one another. She seemed to have forgotten very quickly just how compatible they had been—and not just in bed. This about-turn in his thinking was perfectly acceptable to Matt. Things were different now. Instead of trying to spot the possible downsides, she should be trying to see the definite upsides. As he was! He was prepared to make any necessary sacrifices. Why shouldn't she?

'I could stay on in Manhattan…'

'That's non-negotiable.'

'Maybe live with Claire until I find myself a flat and a job.'

'Have you heard a word I said?' Matt looked at her incredulously. 'You won't be working. There will be no need. Nor will you be rooming with your sister.' His face registered distaste. 'If you're hell-bent on not accepting my proposal, then a suitable place will be found. Somewhere close. *Very* close.' He scowled, still disgruntled with the way his plans had been derailed. 'With regards to my work, I know that you want to contribute financially, but there will be no need for you to think that I come as part of the package.'

'Why are you so determined to put obstacles in my way!'

'I'm not putting obstacles in your way, Matt. You accused me of having ulterior motives in going to bed with you…' Tess felt her voice wobble, just thinking back to that hurtful accusation.

'I apologise,' he inserted quickly. 'You have to understand that it's my nature to be suspicious. I was just taking a step back and voicing possibilities.'

'There's no point trying to backtrack now,' Tess told him stiffly. 'You said what you said in the heat of the moment but you meant every word. I'm not happy about the thought of living off you, and I won't do it.'

'Most women would kill for what you're being offered,' Matt intoned with intense irritation.

'I'm not *most women*, so don't you go bundling me up in the same parcel as everyone else!'

'What job are you going to get?'

'I want to go into teaching. I told you. I'll investigate the process.'

Matt instantly determined that, whatever the process was, he would make sure that he decided it. He would not envisage a life with his child being raised separately while Tess vanished off to teach other people's children. She should be with her own, keeping the home fires burning for him, looking after Samantha…

It was a comfortable image. Seductive even.

'Now—' Tess stood up '—I feel really drained. It's

been stressful for me too, believe it or not, and I have a lot of things to be thinking about. So if you don't mind I'm going to head back to the apartment. I'll be in touch with you tomorrow.'

He was being dismissed! Control had been completely wrested from his possession, and for once he was in the position of having to grit his teeth and take it.

'What time? I could send Stanton for you. We can have lunch. Dinner, if you prefer. There's still a lot to discuss…'

'I'll…I'll let you know…' Tess said vaguely. She had so much to think about. Was she doing the right thing? He had offered marriage. Was it fair to the baby growing inside her that she turned him down? Her head felt as though it would burst.

They both needed space to think, and she wouldn't let him call the shots. That was a dangerous road which she had already travelled. Matt Strickland didn't love her. He never had and he never would, and the arrival of a baby wouldn't change that. And without love how could she marry him? That thought infused her with strength.

'Perhaps the day after tomorrow,' she amended. 'And then we can meet up and talk this over like two adults. Once we've done that, we can start sorting out the practicalities. This sort of thing happens to loads of people. We're not unique. We can both deal with it and move on.'

CHAPTER NINE

TESS returned to her sister's apartment to find that nothing in life ever went according to plan. The answer-machine was blinking furiously and there were five messages. Four were from her sister and one was from her mum. Her mother's message, delivered in an awkward, stilted voice—her *I'm-leaving-a-message* voice—informed her that her father had been rushed to hospital with a suspected heart attack. 'Everything will be fine, we're sure,' her mother had added as an afterthought. 'No need for you to come back home early. Our Mary is on top of things. It's wonderful to have a doctor in the family.'

The remaining messages were from Claire, repeating what their mother had communicated and adding that she was at the airport and would be in the air by the time Tess got the message. Then she demanded, 'Don't you ever answer your cell phone?'

There were eight missed calls and several text messages. Her cell phone had been innocently forgotten and was still in the kitchen, on charge.

The thoughts that had been driving her crazy on the trip back to the apartment now flew out of her head, replaced by panic. Her father was *never* ill. In fact, Tess didn't think that he had ever registered with a doctor—or if he had he had been a once-in-a-lifetime patient. If her mother had seen fit to call, then it must be serious. That was the path her logic took. It also advised her to get on the next flight out.

She flung some things in a hand luggage bag, and on the way to the airport reflected that getting out of the country for a while was probably the best thing that could have happened. Away from Manhattan, she would have time to think in peace. She would phone Matt in a few days and arrange to meet with him just as soon as she judged that her father was fit and fine.

Not seeing him would be the biggest act of kindness she could give herself, because seeing him earlier on had just reconfirmed what she had already known. He wreaked havoc with her peace of mind. The second she laid eyes on him it was as if an electric charge had been plunged into her, and it didn't matter how much she tried to think herself out of feeling that way, she was helpless against his impact.

Some time away from him—even a few days—would allow her to build up some defences. She would have to face the unappealing reality that her life was going to change for ever. Not only would she have a permanent tie with Matt, but she would be condemned to follow the outcome of his choices through the years. She would have to watch from the outside as he became involved with other women, shared his life with them, introduced them to Samantha and to their own child. However much he wanted to take on responsibility, she'd had to release him from a sacrifice that would have destroyed them both, and it wouldn't be long before his relationship with her became purely functional.

She would have to learn to deal with that. She would get a job when the baby was born. Not immediately. First she would check out colleges and see what might be required of her. Those weeks of teaching Samantha had bolstered her confidence. She would start her academic climb with a positive outcome in sight. In time, she would get a job and meet someone else. Someone more suitable.

When she began to think about this mystery man, waiting just around a mythical corner, her thoughts became vague, and she had to stop herself from making the sweeping assumption that no one could ever possibly compete with Matt.

As soon as she landed in Ireland she phoned her mother who, like her, had a habit of forgetting her mobile phone—leaving it on counters, in the bedroom, sometimes on top of the television. Because, 'If it's important, whoever it is will call the proper phone.' There was no reply.

Exhausted after her long flight over, and greeted with a damp, unappealing Ireland which seemed so much quieter and so much less vibrant after the excitement of New York, Tess took a cab back to her home.

The buzz of the city was well and truly left behind as the taxi meandered along the highway and then trundled along narrow streets surrounded by great stretches of countryside, as though the cab driver had all the time in the world.

He talked incessantly, and Tess made a few agreeable

noises while allowing her thoughts to wander like flotsam and jetsam on an ocean current. She pictured her father lying grey-faced and vulnerable on a hospital bed. Mary would know exactly what was going on, and would give her a more realistic assessment than either her mother or Claire. When she thought of her father being seriously ill she began to perspire, and switched her thoughts to her own problem. Although she would be seeing her entire family, she would not be able to breathe a word about her condition. She would have to wait until things calmed down a bit—then she would break the news. The very last thing either of her parents needed was yet more stress. Maybe she would wait until she returned to Manhattan. She hoped her mother wouldn't expect her to stay on.

It was yet another possible complication that she once again shied away from facing. Life as she once knew it now seemed simple in comparison, but looking around her as the taxi drew into the small village where she had, until recently, lived with her parents, Tess wondered how she hadn't itched to fly the coop long ago. Everything was so *small* and so *static*. They drove past the village hall, the shops, the cinema. Several miles away there was a bigger town, where she had always gone with her friends, but even that seemed rural and placid in comparison to the vigour of Manhattan.

The house was empty when she arrived, but signs of occupation were everywhere to be seen. Mary's jacket hung on the banister. Claire's bag had been dumped in the hall and lay half open, with items of clothing spilling out.

The immediacy of the situation grabbed Tess by

the throat, and all thoughts of Matt were temporarily jettisoned.

The next few hours were a blur of activity. She was deeply, deeply exhausted, but her body continued operating on autopilot. She contacted Claire, then drove her mother's car to the hospital—and that felt very strange after a diet of public transport, taxis and Matt's private chauffeur.

'He just complained of feeling a bit out of breath,' her mother whispered, drawing her to one to whisper. 'The old fool.' Her eyes had begun watering but she soldiered on and blinked her tears away. 'Never had a day's illness in his life, so he didn't want me to call the doctor. Thank the Lord I did! They say it's just a scare. He's going to be fine. But he'll have to give up some of his favourite foods. He's not going to like that. You know your dad.'

It was late by the time Tess's body finally caught up with. One minute she was chatting with her sisters and her mother in the kitchen, then she was having her shower, slipping into a nightie, and then her head hit the pillow and she disappeared into sleep as though tranquillised.

And that continued to be the case for the next three days. She settled into a routine of sorts—back in her old bedroom, sharing the bathroom with Mary and Claire and bickering with them about the length of time they took whenever they ran a bath. Her father was improving steadily and had begun to complain about the hospital food, which seemed a good sign.

Lurking at the back of the gentle chaos and the cosiness of the familiar was Matt's dark, brooding presence, and the pressing situation with which they had yet to deal. But every time Tess reached for the phone to call him her hand faltered and she began sweating, and then she'd postpone the conversation which she knew would inevitably have to be made. After the second day he began to leave messages on her mobile, and missed calls were registered. Tess decided to give it until the weekend to get in touch. The weekend would mark five days out of contact.

Mary would be returning to London and Claire would be going with her, taking a few days off to remain in the country and using the opportunity to import Tom, so that they could do some shopping and also meet the parents if she deemed that her father was up to it. She had already e-mailed her resignation and seemed to have no regrets about losing her high-flying job in Manhattan because Tom would be transferring to London. Between her father's improving health and Claire's exciting news Tess was happy to sideline herself in the background, where she could nurse her own worries in peace.

Which was precisely what she was doing in her room, with her tiny, very old television turned on very low, telling her about unexpected flooding in Cornwall, when her mobile went and an unknown number was displayed.

At the very height of his frustration Matt had invested in a new phone, with a new number, because after days of trying without success he could think of no other way of getting in contact with her.

He'd hesitated to telephone her sister. What excuse could he possibly give? Tess had been adamant that she would break the news to her family in her own time.

Already dealing with having his perfectly formulated plan to marry her turned on its head, the last thing he needed would be to arm her with more grounds for grievance.

Over a period of three days his mood had travelled on a one-way road from poor to appalling. He couldn't get her out of his mind. Then he'd begun to worry. What if she had been taken ill? Been in an accident? Was lying somewhere in a hospital, unable to get in touch? The surge of sickening emotion that had filled him at the thought of that had been shocking—although, as he had shakily reminded himself, perfectly understandable given her condition. He was a man of honour. He *would* be shaken to the core at the thought of the mother of his child falling ill and being unable to get in touch with him.

But before he began ringing round the hospitals in the area he'd had the last-minute brainwave of buying a new phone—one with a new and unrecognisable number—just in case she simply wasn't answering his calls.

The second he heard her voice at the other end of the line he felt a spasm of red-hot anger envelop him like a mist. He realised that he had been *worried sick* about her.

'So you *are* alive,' were his opening words.

On the other side of the Atlantic, Tess sat up in bed. The sound of his voice was like a shot of adrenaline, delivered intravenously.

'Matt…I've been meaning to give you a call.'

'Really? When?' It was just as well that she wasn't within strangling distance, he thought with barely suppressed fury. 'In case you haven't noticed, I've made several hundred calls to you over the past few days. *Where the hell are you?* I've been to the apartment four times and no one has been there!'

'I needed to have a little time to myself.' She glanced around her furtively, half expecting to see him materialise out of thin air, so forceful was his personality even over a telephone thousands of miles away.

'I'm sick to death of hearing what *you* need!' He had to stop himself from roaring down the line. There was no place for anything less than civilised behaviour in their situation, but the woman brought out a side to him that he hadn't known existed and one which he found difficult to control. Not even with Catrina, at the very height of their dysfunctional marriage, when revelations had been pouring out from the woodwork like termites, had he felt so uncontrollably responsive. Where with Catrina he had taken refuge from his problems by burying himself in his work, with Tess that was no solution. However hard he tried, it was impossible to focus. 'Running away isn't the solution! Where *are* you?'

'I'm...' Two things stopped her from telling him the truth. The first was the knowledge that to confess that she was on the other side of the Atlantic, having taken off without bothering to let him know, would make him even angrier than he already sounded. The second was the fact that she *couldn't* let him know where she was. He was her problem in America, and with her father still recuperating there was no way that she wanted him to intrude and possibly risk jeopardising her father's recovery. How would her parents react if he phoned the house and gave the game away? Let slip that she was pregnant? Single and pregnant by a man who wasn't going to be her husband? Her parents would have to be gently eased into that, and this was not the right time.

'I'm out of New York. Just for…for a few days. I know we have stuff to talk about, and I'll give you a call just as soon as I return.'

'Where. Are. You?'

'I'm…'

'If you don't tell me where you are,' he said in a calmer voice, 'then I'll do some investigative work and find out for myself. You would be surprised how fast I can get information when I want it.'

'I told you—'

'Yes, I know what you told me, and I'm choosing to ignore it.'

'I'm back home,' Tess confessed, 'in Ireland. My dad got rushed into hospital and I just had to get to the airport and fly over.'

Matt paused. 'Rushed into hospital with what?'

'A heart attack scare. Look, I'm sorry—'

'And is he all right?' Matt interrupted tersely.

'On the mend. We're all very relieved.'

'Why didn't you say so in the first place? No. Better question. Why didn't you answer one of my five hundred calls and *tell* me that?'

'I had a lot on my mind…and I wanted to have some space to think…'

Across the water, alarm bells started ringing.

Matt was in no doubt that her initial reaction to hearing about her father would have been to hop on the first flight out. Although he was close enough to his parents, they had always been highly social and very much involved in their own lives. Tess, on the other hand, was fiercely attached to her parents and her sisters. He assumed that she would not have broken the news about her pregnancy to them—not given the circumstances.

But *why* hadn't she picked up any of his phone calls? Or returned any of them?

Space to think amongst her tightly knit family unit, back on her home turf, allied itself, in his head, with her desire to find happiness with someone else. It was not a happy alliance. With the comforting familiarity of her village around her, how long before she started contemplating the prospect of foregoing the stress of the unknown in New York? He was certain that her parents would react kindly to her pregnancy. Perhaps a small moral lecture, but they would weather the news and immediately provide support.

New York would fast become a distant memory. She might nurse some scruples about running away, but how long before she recalled the adverse way in which he had reacted to news of the pregnancy? How long before she started thinking of his insinuations about the financial benefits of having his baby—his implication that she might have engineered an agreeable financial nest egg for herself? Would she take time to step back and consider *his* side of the story? See where *his* perfectly understandable concerns stemmed from?

Not for the first time, Matt wondered why she couldn't have been one of the scores of willing women who would have been *overjoyed* at a marriage proposal from him and the financial security for life it entailed. But then the thought of Tess falling into line with one of those women was laughable.

She was telling him now about how much it was helping, being back in Ireland.

'So when exactly do you expect to be back here?' he cut in. Now that his brain had taken off on another tangent, like a runaway horse, he was alert to that shade of hesitation before she answered, and was composed and understanding when she mumbled something about as soon as she could—though she couldn't very well leave her mum on her own immediately. Not with Mary and Claire both gone.

He rang off shortly after.

There was a considerable amount of work for him to do. Meetings with important clients, bankers, lawyers. It only took a few phone calls to rearrange that situation.

His next call was to his mother, who would cover for him at home in his absence, ensuring that Samantha had a familiar face when he wasn't around. She had only just started at her new school and, whilst everything seemed to be progressing with startling ease, he still felt better knowing that she would return to the apartment and someone who actually had a vested interest in whether she did her homework or not.

Then he called Samantha, who had to be fetched out of her class and was breathless when she picked up. Amidst the turmoil, her moment of disappointment when he broke the news that he would be out of town for a couple of nights was a light on the horizon.

His calls completed, Matt informed his secretary to get him on the first flight out to Ireland.

He was thinking on his feet—something he was excellent at. He left his office with instructions for his flight details to be texted to him within the hour, and then he was heading back to his apartment, packing the minimum of things, fired up by an urgency to *act*.

He didn't know whether Tess would have run away to find her space to think had she not been called on an emergency, but now that she *had* left the country he wasn't going to hang around to find out whether her return was on the cards.

Tess Kelly was unpredictable in the extreme. There were also hormones rushing through her body. He wasn't completely clueless about pregnancy. Under the influence of her hormones, she was capable of pretty much *any* rash decision!

As fresh thoughts superimposed themselves on already existing ones, his decision to go to Ireland seemed better and better by the second.

Having checked out the paperwork which she had dutifully filled in at her time of employment, he had easily ascertained her parents' address. The only question was whether he would show up unannounced on the doorstep, or get to see her via a more roundabout route.

Respecting the situation concerning her father, Matt arrived in Ireland intending to settle himself into a local hotel and then consider his next step forward. His intention was blocked when he discovered that there was no hotel in the village, which was much smaller than he might have expected.

'Where *is* the nearest hotel?' He impatiently directed his question to the taxi driver, who seemed quite pleased to have delivered his fare to the middle of nowhere.

'Depends on what sort of hotel you're looking for.'

Fed up, Matt decided to take his chances on going directly to her parents' house, and he handed the driver a slip of paper on which he had scribbled the address. He would deal with whatever problem arose from his decision with his customary aplomb.

It was a matter of fifteen minutes before the taxi was pulling up in front of a Victorian house with a pristine front garden and enough acreage to just about avoid being overlooked by the neighbours.

The flight had been long and tiresome, even in first class, but Matt was raring to go. He felt as though he had spent the past few days sitting on his hands, and that just wasn't his style. He was confrontational by nature.

He was prepared for anything and anyone as he pressed the doorbell and waited.

Not for a moment did it occur to him that no one would be home, and the sound of hurrying footsteps rewarded him for his confidence.

Tess had been looking forward to a bit of peace and quiet. Claire had left not an hour ago, and shortly after that her mother had gone to the hospital, leaving Tess to tidy up the house, which hadn't been touched properly since her father had been taken into hospital.

She had no idea who could be at the door. She debated not answering and hoping that the caller would eventually get the message and disappear, but she couldn't do it.

Pulling open the door, dressed in old clothes which she had worn as a teenager—faded track pants and an old tee shirt that should have been thrown out a long time ago—Tess half wished that she *had* ignored the bell, although for a few heart-stopping seconds, she didn't quite believe her eyes.

Matt was larger than life—dramatic against the crisp Irish scenery and the quietness of the rural backdrop.

'You look surprised to see me.'

He remained on the doorstep and looked at her. Her caramel-coloured hair was pulled up into a scruffy ponytail, and her clothes looked as though they had seen better days, but even so he still found it a strain to keep his hands to himself. He always knew when she wasn't wearing a bra, and she wasn't wearing one now. He could make out the slight hang of her breasts, and the tiny peaks where her nipples were jutting against the soft jersey of her tee shirt.

'Are you here on your own?' he asked, when she made no attempt to break the silence. 'I didn't want to crash land on you, Tess, but I felt that it might be better all round if I came here instead of waiting for you to return to America.'

'I haven't told anyone about us!' she breathed. 'There's no one at home now, but it would have been a disaster if you'd come two hours ago!'

'Oh, I don't think so,' Matt drawled, running out of patience. 'Sooner or later everyone is going to have to know, and ducking and pretending that that time isn't going to come won't solve anything. Are you going to invite me in?' He held out his hand and gave her a duty-free carrier bag from the airport. 'A book for your father—it's the latest one by that guy you told me that he likes—and a scarf for your mother.'

Tess stepped aside and watched warily as he entered the hallway. As happened everywhere he went, he dominated his surroundings and she couldn't wrest her eyes away from him. The sight of one of his designer holdalls in his hand broke the spell.

'How long are you planning on staying?' she asked, dismayed.

'I'm staying until you're ready to come back to America with me.'

'You mean you came all the way here to escort me back to New York? Like a kid who has run away from home?' Annoyed with herself, because her excitement levels had rocketed the second she had clapped eyes on him, thereby proving that all her hard work over the past few days had been for nothing, Tess was ready to pick a fight. Did he think that he could do just as he pleased? What did that herald for their future? Would she be relegated to being told what to do at a moment's notice, just because he could? Rich, beautiful Catrina from another powerful family had been able to assert her own terms, even if they had been unfair. *She*, on the other hand, had no such power behind her, so where exactly would she stand?

'Well, you may be here longer than you think.' Tess folded her arms. 'Claire and Mary have both left for London, and someone has to stay with Mum until Dad's back home. Maybe even longer. Who knows? She's going to need lots of help.'

'And you're going to volunteer for the post without breathing a word to either of them about your condition? I can't allow that.'

'You can't *allow* it?' Tess looked at him incredulously. 'Since when do you have a say in what I do and don't do?'

'We've been over this.' So he *had* been right to get on a plane and pursue her. She had no intention of hurrying back to New York. 'And I can't allow it because you're in no kind of condition to start doing heavy manual chores around the house. I will ensure that there is someone here to take the strain off your mother—'

'You'll do nothing of the kind!' Tess cried. 'She won't even know that you've been here!'

'And how do you figure on keeping me a secret?' Matt grated. 'Are you going to lock me away in a room somewhere and feed me scraps of food through a hole in the door? Because I'm telling you right now that's the only way you're going to be able to keep me out of sight. I didn't come here to have a fight with you!'

'No, you came to cart me away!' *You don't care about me*, she thought, as furious resentment rose to the surface and threatened to spill over. *You would have happily turned your back and never seen me again, but now here you are, suddenly concerned for my welfare because I happen to be pregnant with your child!*

'If needs be,' Matt confirmed with implacable steel. 'In the process, I intend to stay until I meet your parents and tell them what's going on.'

Tess blanched. 'You can't. Dad's not well.'

'What do you think will happen if you break the news to him? I'm tired of playing games with you over this, Tess. You're twenty-three years old. You're sexually active. You got pregnant. Which bit of that do you imagine would affect them most?'

Tess chewed her lip and looked away.

'Well?' Matt pressed. 'Do you think that they will

collapse on the spot if they find out that you've had a relationship.'

'It wasn't a relationship.' She knew exactly where the sticking point was with her parents—her charming, old-fashioned parents, with their old-fashioned ways and gentle moral code. 'They won't like the fact that I'm pregnant…they won't like it that I'm going to be a single mother. Neither of them can deal with that shock right now. You have to trust me.'

'I'm staying, Tess—and you can always spare them the shock of your being an unmarried mother, can't you? Think about it. Think about how happy they would be if they knew that their daughter was pregnant but was going to *marry* the father of her child…'

CHAPTER TEN

TESS looked at Matt in disbelief. 'I need to sit down,' she said shakily. She walked on legs that felt like wood into the comfortable sitting room and sank onto a squashy sofa, tucking her feet under her.

For a few moments Matt strolled through the room, barely noticing the pictures in the frames, the ornaments, all the reminders of a life greatly enhanced by children. His attention was focused on Tess. She looked small and vulnerable, huddled on the sofa, but Matt wasn't going to allow himself to feel sorry for her.

She had fled to Ireland without bothering to call him, she had ignored every phone call and message he had left for her, and she had as good as admitted that she had no intention of hurrying back to New York.

'That's blackmail.' She raised huge, accusing eyes to his and his mouth tightened.

'It's problem-solving. You're terrified that your parents are going to be disappointed in you, and I'm showing you that there's no need for that.'

'I've spent ages telling you why it would be a bad idea.'

'Yes. I heard all the reasons you churned out.' He sat heavily on the sofa, depressing it with his weight, and

Tess shifted awkwardly to avoid physical contact. 'You don't see the need to marry me just because we made a mistake. Life's too short to be trapped in a marriage for the wrong reasons. You want to spread your wings and find your soul mate.'

'You're twisting everything I said.'

'Tell me which bit you think I've got wrong. The trapped bit? The soul mate bit? Were you *ever* going to return to Manhattan? Or did you come back here with good intentions only to decide that you would erase me out of your life?'

'Of *course* I was going to return to New York! I'm not irresponsible! I want you to have a real bond with this child.'

'You're one hundred percent irresponsible!' Matt snapped. He looked at her with glowering, scowling intensity. 'You refuse to marry me. You refuse to acknowledge that a child needs both parents. You witnessed first-hand the hell I went through gaining Samantha's trust—trust that should have been mine by right but was destroyed by a vengeful ex-wife.'

'I can't bear to think of you putting up with me for the sake of a child.' Tess defied the suffocating force of his personality to put across her point of view. She thought of her parents and how they would react to the thought of her living a single, unsupported life in New York. Based on their experience, children should be born into a united home. How would they ever understand that love and marriage didn't necessarily go together? They were savvy enough when it came to the rest of the world, but she had a sinking feeling that they would be a lot less savvy when it came to their own offspring.

The fact that Claire was excitedly due to be married to the man of her dreams would make it all the harder for them to understand how she, Tess, had managed to become embroiled in the situation that she had.

Matt was offering her a way out, and for a split second she desperately wanted to take it. It wouldn't be ideal—no one could say that—but it would solve a lot of problems.

She pulled herself up short when she remembered how her cotton-candy daydreams and pointless, optimistic fantasising had landed her where she was now. She had fallen in love with him and dared to hope that time would work it's magic and miraculously *make* him love her. It hadn't, and she would be a complete fool to forget that. Marry him, she told herself sternly, and she would witness the slow build-up of his indifference. He would have affairs, even if he kept them under wraps for the sake of maintaining a phoney front, and she would never, ever be able to give herself a chance at finding someone who could care for her.

'Don't try and get into my head, Tess.'

'I know you.'

'I'm willing to make the sacrifice. Why aren't you? You were happy with me once,' he said brusquely. 'We got along. It's ridiculous for you to assume that we can't make a go of it.'

'If we could have made a go of it—if you had *wanted* to make a go of it—you would have asked me to stay. You would have been prepared to make a go of it then.'

Matt hesitated. 'This is too big for wounded pride

to come into the equation. Anyway, maybe I made a mistake.'

'Mistake? What kind of mistake?' She looked at him suspiciously. She had dared to hope so many times that the prospect of daring to hope again was literally exhausting. 'Since when does Matt Strickland *ever* make mistakes?' she muttered, and he gave her a crooked smile that made her heart flip over. 'I don't say that as a compliment,' she qualified quickly, before that smile made her start to lose ground. 'It's important to make mistakes. People learn from their mistakes. I made mistakes growing up. I've learnt from them.'

'Did you make a mistake with me?'

Tess flushed. 'If I could turn back time, I—'

'That's not what I'm asking. I'm asking if you think you made a mistake with me. I don't want an answer based on hypothesis.'

He was no closer to her now. In fact, he was leaning back, looking at her with brooding, narrowed eyes, and still she felt as though she was being touched.

'Because I don't think *I* made a mistake with *you*. I think the mistake I made was to let you go.'

Suddenly the air seemed close and the room too small. The breath caught in her throat and her skin was on fire.

'Don't you dare!' She stood up, trembling, and walked towards the window. Outside, the scene was peaceful. The carefully tended garden was ablaze with flowers. However, Tess was oblivious to the colourful summer landscape. Her heart was beating so hard that if she held her breath she was sure she would be able to hear it.

When she turned around it was to find him standing so close to her that she pressed herself against the window-ledge. His proximity brought her close to a state of panic. She trusted *him*. She just didn't trust *herself*.

'Don't dare...*what*? Come close to you? Why not?' He shoved his hands into his pockets. If he didn't, he knew what he would do. He would reach out and touch her, maybe just tuck that stray strand of hair behind her ear. Hell, her eyes were wide and panicked, and he hated seeing her like this. He clenched his jaw and kept his hands firmly tucked away. 'Why fight me?' he muttered, and dark colour slashed his cheekbones. 'Why fight *this*?'

'I don't know what you're talking about, and I don't need you to try and undermine me. I know what you're doing.'

'Tell me. What *am* I doing?'

'Everything it takes to get what you want,' Tess heard herself say with unaccustomed bitterness. 'You've come here so that you can take me back to New York because you don't trust me. I'm sorry I didn't phone you, and I'm sorry I didn't answer your messages, but I've needed to take a little time out and I've been worried sick with Dad being in hospital. Not that you care. The only thing you care about is making sure that I'm in place, and you'll do whatever it takes to get me there—even if it means blackmailing me into doing what you want. You know what it could do to my parents in the situation they're in if you dump this news on them, but you'd go right ahead and do it if you thought it would get you what you want! And you expect me to *want* to commit myself to you? When everything you do just confirms that you're arrogant and ruthless and only care about what you want?' She drew in a deep breath and braced herself to continue. 'Don't even think of telling me that you made a mistake throwing away what we had!' Her voice was shrill and unforgiving. 'It's easy to say that now. Do you really think that I'd believe you?'

'You're upsetting yourself.'

'I'm not upsetting myself! *You're* upsetting *me*.'

'I don't want to do that. I…I never want to do that.' With an effort, Matt pushed himself away from her and returned to sit on the sofa. Like a slow motion sequence in a film, every mistake he had made with her rose up with reproving clarity.

He had been attracted to her, and without a second thought he had seduced her into his bed. He had accepted the gift of her virginity without bothering to question the devil in the detail, and then, when she had suggested remaining in New York, he had run a mile. Conditioned to identify himself through his work, and accustomed to always ensuring that it was placed at the top of the agenda, he had reacted to her reasonable requests about where their relationship was heading by backing away.

To compound his sins he had greeted news of her pregnancy with suspicion—only to further raise her guard and drive her away by insisting on trying to determine what she should do and what she shouldn't.

Had he even *once* thought about stepping back and taking stock of how he actually felt?

Not in the habit of doubting his ability to manage situations, Matt was shaken to the core at the realisation that he had blown it. She might tremble the second he got near her, but a physical response wasn't enough. It had never been enough. And yet he knew that if he told her that now she wouldn't believe a word he said, and he couldn't blame her.

Tess looked at him uneasily. For once his deepening silence didn't seem to indicate anything ulterior. He wasn't even looking at her. He was staring into space and his expression was unreadable.

She took a hesitant step away from the window, but it was only when she was standing in front of him that he raised his eyes to hers.

'I've screwed up,' he said bluntly. He raked his fingers into his hair and lowered his eyes. 'Of course I'm not going to blackmail you into anything.'

'You're not?'

'Sit. Please? And that's not a command. It's a request.'

Tess, caught off guard by this strangely unsettling and subdued side to him, perched primly on the edge of the sofa, ready and willing to take flight at a moment's notice—although her hands wanted to reach out, and she wanted to lace her fingers through his. Frankly, she had to resist the powerful urge to do anything necessary to bring a smile to his lips, even if that smile was laced with cynicism. This was not a Matt she was accustomed to seeing, and it disconcerted her.

'You think I'm trying to take advantage of you? I'm not.' Matt felt as though he was standing on the edge of a precipice, arms outstretched, about to fling himself over the side in the wild hope that he would be caught by a safety net. He also felt very, very calm. 'I've done so many things wrong that I don't even know where to begin to try and explain myself, and I fully understand that you probably won't believe a word I say to you. Frankly, I wouldn't blame you. I entered into a relationship with you for the sex—pure and simple. I've been bitten once, and I've lived my life since then making damn sure that I wouldn't be bitten again. Every woman I've ever been with since Catrina has been like Vicky. It was easy never to become involved. My personal relationships were effectively, just extensions of my working life, with sex thrown in.'

Tess, all ears, found that she was holding her breath. With his walls breaking down, this was a vulnerable Matt laying his soul bare. She knew that instinctively, and she wasn't going to break the spell. Every word wrenched out of him was like manna to her ears. If she wasn't being hopelessly enthralled, she would be slightly ashamed.

'I should have questioned what it was I saw in you when you came along, but I didn't. I've always had absolute, unwavering control in my personal life. How could I expect that what I had with you would be any different?'

'And it was? Really? How different?' Tess cleared her throat and blushed sheepishly. 'It's important, you know—to…um…let it all out…'

'In that case, it's very kind of you to let me talk,' Matt murmured wryly. '*Very* different, in answer to your question. You made me a very different person. I did things with you that were all firsts—although at the time I hardly recognised it. I stopped work for you. Yes, I went to meetings—I organised deals, I met with the usual lawyers and bankers and hedge fund directors—but for the first time in my life I couldn't wait to get back to the apartment. I managed to persuade myself that that was because my relationship with my daughter was finally beginning to take shape. Of course that was part of the reason. You were the other part. You made leaving work behind easy.'

Tess allowed herself a little smile of pure joy, because whatever came out in the wash, nothing would ever erase the warm pleasure that his admission was giving her, and like a kid in a toy shop she didn't want the experience to end. When would she have the opportunity to visit that place again?

'When you asked to prolong our relationship, I reacted out of habit and instinct. Both told me to walk away. I didn't bother to question it, and once it had been done pride entered the equation. But you never left my head. It was as though you had become stuck there. No matter what I did, you followed me everywhere I went—a silent, nagging reminder of what I'd thrown away.'

'But you would never have said a word if I hadn't shown up in your office and told you that I was pregnant,' Tess said ruefully.

'Wouldn't I?' Matt caught her eyes and held her gaze. 'I'm inclined to think that I would have. I'm inclined to think that I would have been right here, in this place, doing what I'm doing now, even if you hadn't made life so much easier for me by falling pregnant.'

'But it was unplanned. You were furious. You *blamed* me!'

'I've never had any lessons in being in love. How was I to know what to say and how to react?'

'Being in love?' Her voice trembled, and her hands trembled too as he took them in his.

He stroked her fingers with his thumb. Sincerity blazed from his eyes. 'If I'd ever known true love,' he admitted gruffly, 'I might have recognised the symptoms. But nothing prepared me for you, Tess. Looking back, I can see that Catrina was just an expectation I fulfilled without thinking too hard about it. You were the unexpected. You crash-landed into my life and everything changed overnight. I didn't come here to take you away against your will, and I'm sorry that that was the impression I ended up giving.'

'You love me?' She repeated it with wonder, trying it out on her tongue for size and liking the way it felt. Too good to be true. But when she looked at him she knew that he meant every word of what he had said. 'I love *you*,' she whispered. 'I slept with you because I loved you. You were everything my head told me I shouldn't want, but you crash-landed into my life as well...'

'I want to marry you, Tess. I don't want to marry you because you're having our baby. I want to marry you because my life isn't complete unless you're in it. I want to go to sleep with you beside me every night, and I want to wake up in the morning with you right next to me.'

With a sigh of contentment, Tess crawled onto his lap and closed her eyes, happy to be enfolded in his warmth and to feel his fingers gently stroke her hair.

'I've never been so happy in my entire life,' she confessed. 'I think I might cry, given half a chance.'

'Will you marry me as soon as possible?' he breathed. 'I know you probably don't want to take the attention away from your sister, but I don't know how long I can wait. I want you to flash my ring on your finger so that every man out there knows that he's not to come within ten feet of you unless specifically given permission.'

Tess laughed into his shoulder, and then wriggled so that she could look up at him.

'That's ultra-possessive...'

'I'm an ultra-possessive man,' he growled, 'and don't ever forget it.' At last he felt free to touch her, to feel the wonder of her body that was slowly going to be transformed with his baby in it. He pushed his hands up under her tee shirt and groaned as the rounded curves of her breasts filled them. He stroked her nipples, and the familiar feel of them hardening under his touch was beyond erotic.

'Is there any chance that a family member might surprise me in the middle of making love to you?' he questioned in a shaky undertone. 'Because if there is, then we're going to have to get to your bedroom quickly. I love you and I want you and I need you. It feels like it's been years...'

Upstairs, on her small double bed, they made love with sweet, lingering slowness. To Matt it really did feel as though it had been years since he had touched her, even though it had been only a matter of a couple of weeks.

He touched her everywhere. He kissed and nuzzled the breasts that would enlarge over the months, and suckled on nipples that would darken and distend. When he came into her, her slippery sheath brought him to an almost immediate orgasm. Never had making love been such a liberating experience—but, then again, never had a woman unlocked him in the way she had…

They were married less than two months later. It was a quiet and very romantic ceremony, at the local church where her parents had been members of the congregation for ever. Matt's parents and a handful of close friends made the journey, and of course Samantha was the centre of attention and as excitable as it was possible to be.

Tess had never doubted that her parents would embrace Matt as a member of their family, and they did. She was more surprised and thrilled that his parents were just as warm and welcoming towards her. Maybe it was because they could see the devotion on their son's face whenever he looked at her, and the love on his daughter's face at the prospect of Tess becoming her stepmother.

Small but subtle changes took place over the ensuing months. They continued to live in Matt's vast penthouse apartment, which was convenient for Samantha's school, but they also bought a country house of their own, and spent most weekends there. Tess hadn't abandoned the prospect of a career in teaching, although she was now going to wait until the baby was born and then take everything slowly and in her stride. The fact that both Matt and Samantha had one hundred percent belief in her was a huge encouragement.

Tess had never thought that such happiness was possible, and her feelings of contentment must have transmitted themselves to her baby, for little Isobel was born without drama. Eight and a half pounds of apple-cheeked, green-eyed, black-haired, good-natured little girl.

She could only smile and agree when Matt, as he was fond of doing, told them that at long last he was where he had always wanted to be—surrounded by beautiful females who had finally succeeded in domesticating him.

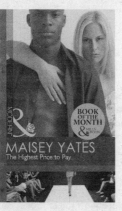

711/01b

FROM DIRT TO DIAMONDS

by Julia James

Thea owes her future to a lucky encounter years ago with gorgeous Greek tycoon Angelos Petrakos. Angelos can't forget how she used him—and he'll stop at nothing to bring her down. Even seduction…

FIANCÉE FOR ONE NIGHT

by Trish Morey

Leo Zamos persuades his virtual PA Eve Carmichael to act as his fake fiancée at a business dinner. Leo assumes that Eve will be as neat and professional as her work, but Eve's every bit as tempting as her namesake…

AFTER THE GREEK AFFAIR

by Chantelle Shaw

The only woman billionaire Loukas Christakis trusts is his soon-to-be-married little sister. He's reluctantly allowed designer Belle Andersen to make the wedding dress on his private island—where he can keep an eye on her!

UNDER THE BRAZILIAN SUN

by Catherine George

No one has tempted reclusive ex racing champion Roberto de Sousa out from his mansion. Dr Katherine Lister is there to value a rare piece of art. But under Roberto's sultry gaze she feels like a priceless jewel…

On sale from 5th August 2011
Don't miss out!

Available at WHSmith, Tesco, ASDA, Eason and all good bookshops

www.millsandboon.co.uk

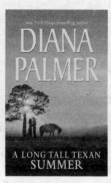